Savannah GREY

CLIFF MᶜNISH

Savannah
GREY

✿ carolrhoda LAB

First American edition published in 2011 by Carolrhoda Lab™. Published by arrangement with Orion Children's Books, a division of Orion Publishing Group Ltd., London, England

Carolrhoda Lab™
An imprint of Carolrhoda Books
A division of Lerner Publishing Group, Inc.
241 First Avenue North
Minneapolis, MN 55401 U.S.A.

Website address: www.lernerbooks.com

Cover: © iStockphoto.com/VikaValter (main, front), © iStockphoto.com/Heidi Kristensen (floral pattern, front and back). Interior: © iStockphoto.com/VikaValter (title page); © iStockphoto.com/Heidi Kristensen (floral pattern background used throughout).

Library of Congress Cataloging-in-Publication Data

McNish, Cliff.
    Savannah Grey / by Cliff McNish.
        p.   cm.
    Summary: As nature seems to be exerting an overpowering force on the world, a fifteen-year-old English girl learns that she has supernatural powers and discovers her true purpose.
        ISBN: 978–0–7613–7025–3 (trade hard cover : alk. paper)
        [1. Supernatural—Fiction. 2. Nature—Fiction.] I. Title.
    PZ7.M478797Sav 2011
    [Fic]—dc22   2010028137

Manufactured in the United States of America
1 – SB – 12/31/10

TO CHINA MIÉVILLE
FOR REMINDING ME WHY, IN A WORLD
ALREADY OVERFLOWING WITH NOVELS, IT MIGHT
BE WORTH WRITING ONE MORE

PROLOGUE

It was long past midnight when the Horror appeared at the end of Westmoreland Road. No one in the run-down housing project saw it. No one heard as it burst through the washing lines of the poky little yards.

Reaching number thirty-three, Savannah Grey's house, the Horror dropped its star-shaped head on one side, knotted its murderous claws behind its back, and tried to work out the most entertaining way to reach Savannah's bedroom. There were many ways available, but the Horror was young and like all young things, it liked to use its teeth.

Biting a path up the bricks, it anchored its incisors into Savannah's window ledge. Then, thrilled with excitement, it raised its single cobalt-blue eye to the night winds and howled.

The Horror wasn't meant to do that. It wasn't supposed to draw attention to itself. But it had been let loose for the first time in its life and was dying to do everything at once.

A city! Such glorious lights! Never having been unchained for this long before, the Horror's restless claws had been on the move all evening, playing freely and greedily with everything it touched. And on the way to Savannah's, it had chanced upon something that truly made it squeal with delight.

An adolescent girl, dancing in her living room.

Blonde-haired, and dressed in a stretched yellow tutu, she was performing ballet exercises. Seeing the way she whisperingly plotted a path across her carpet—"pas, pas," formal steps punctuated by sudden acrobatic leaps—the Horror had stopped to watch, mesmerized. So this was what humans did in private. They danced! How wondrous! And all the way to Savannah's, the Horror copied what it had seen, shooting over lampposts and rooftops in a series of risky pirouettes and sweeping vaults.

Reaching number thirty-three, the Horror used its subtle tongue to pick the front door lock. It wasn't afraid of being caught. If anyone did so it would simply kill them. Killing was a game, a lovely distraction, to this creature.

Padding merrily on its doglike body, it eased into the hallway, humming softly to itself.

Up the staircase. Onto the landing.

Pitter-patter past the toilet.

Towards the bedrooms.

The Horror stayed silent as it approached Savannah, containing its eagerness. A gland in its throat constantly spouted a yellowish liquid, but it was used to that and made sure none dripped onto the hallway carpet.

One more staircase to go.

Remembering the ballet girl, the Horror smiled. Then, raising its body shakily up on two legs, it crooked its front limbs just so—and waltzed like a dancer with an invisible partner up the last flight of stairs.

Savannah's door was open. A breeze from the landing stirred the wavy ends of her hair. *Glissade*, the Horror thought. Thanks to the ballet girl, it knew several human words now. Without understanding what they meant, it had practiced them on the way here, loving the sounds.

Arrière. Echappé. En dehors. Fouetté. Port de bras. Battement!

Murmuring the last of them, the Horror thrust like a fencer inside Savannah's bedroom. For a moment it simply stood there, its translucent teeth glistening. Then it sprang—an agile, dramatic fling of its hind legs that took it all the way over her duvet. If Savannah had woken, she'd have seen the sharp points of the Horror's head jabbing towards her neck. But Savannah did not wake. She slept on. Her lips were open, the bottom one pouting a little in the relaxed way it always did when she was asleep.

Seeing her eyelids dream-fluttering, the Horror cocked its head on one side. So it was true: humans dreamed as well. Did they dream of monsters the way it dreamed of humans?

Gripping the carpet, it vaulted to the ceiling. There it hung, suspended on suckered pads, its yellow mouth gaping. Savannah exhaled, and the Horror caught a waft of spearmint toothpaste. So excited was it by the smell that it forgot to stay quiet—and noisily sniffed her face.

Fifteen-year-old Savannah woke immediately. Blinking in the darkness, she propped herself up on one arm. What had she heard? A snort, followed by two or three quick scurries.

She stared at the door. Either she'd dreamt the noises, or an animal was in the house. Squirrels? A rat? The possibility that it was something as big as a rat kept her awake for a long time, listening. Eventually, hearing only silence, she dismissed the noises as nothing and turned her head back into the pillow.

Once it was certain she was asleep again, the Horror slipped out from under Savannah's bed. Its lone eye peered down at her. Up close, Savannah didn't look as dangerous as it had been led to believe. Physically she appeared the same as other teenage girls it had been shown pictures of. Or was she?

Disobeying its orders, the Horror teased the sheet away from Savannah's shoulders to reveal her neck. It discovered nothing unusual. Smooth skin. Soft flesh. The hollow of the throat rising gently up to the vocal cords. It was hard for the Horror to accept that inside that throat of hers was a weapon so uniquely powerful that if Savannah ever learned to control it there was virtually nothing which could stand against her.

But the Horror could hear the beginnings of that weapon. Distant noises. Faint rustlings. Distinctive *click-click-clicks*. They drifted in intervals from her lips. And occasionally even more ominous sounds emerged. Heavy booms. Muffled explosions—as if velveted bombs were igniting in the depths of her throat.

The Horror leaned forward. It had an almost irresistible impulse to wake Savannah by biting that throat of hers, but no, it couldn't do that. It wasn't allowed. Its task was merely to listen to the sounds and report the findings to its master, the Ocrassa.

Frustrated—wanting to kill her now, cold and quick, while she slept—the Horror listened for another hour. Then, mewling in silent frustration into its claws, it sped moodily from the house and off into the leaf-blown night.

I

Late afternoon, dreary autumn sunshine, and I was bored. All Sunday I'd been lounging in bed, nursing my sore throat, and generally feeling sorry for myself, when my best friend, Nina Savoy, called.

"Hi, it's me. What you up to?"

The answer was dreaming about monsters again, but Nina never liked the details so I just said, "Nothing."

"Still sick in bed with your throat?"

"Um."

"Well, see if this makes you feel better. We've been invited out. Tori's throwing one of her parties."

"Uh-uh," I protested weakly. "No way I'm going out tonight."

Nina laughed. "Sav, that hurts. It really does. Especially when I've gone to so much trouble to invite along the perfect boy for you."

I groaned. Nina takes it as a personal insult that I've never seriously gone out with anyone yet. When I'm ready, I keep telling her, but she's unstoppable once she gets an idea into her head. The blind date she sprung on me last week with Henry Duke was typical. Henry's a modest, smart, funny boy from my physics class. In fact I'd always liked him, and though I was flustered by having the date dropped on me, I was really enjoying myself until we took our seats at Peckham cinema.

That's when Henry made his *great move*. I knew he was going to do it. From little shufflings of his bum it was obvious what he was up to—edging closer, calculating distances, daring himself. And when he actually found the guts to spread that thin freckled arm of his around my shoulder, and swing in for a quick half-kiss, I must admit that part of me had felt pleased and almost pathetically grateful.

But then I'd pulled away. I'm not sure why. A cold feeling had just swept over me. Ludicrously, instead of meeting up with his mouth, all I'd wanted to do in that moment was stop Henry. Stop him and carefully inspect what was inside his lips. Not exactly the easiest thing to ask a boy just before he gives you his best move.

All of which meant that meeting someone else tonight, especially a stranger, was the last thing I had in mind.

"Gargle something," Nina said, unfazed by my protests. "Staying in bed is what's making you miserable. Anyway, it's midterm break so you can lounge in bed the whole of next week if you want. Trust me, you're definitely going to want to meet this boy."

"Oh yeah?" I grunted.

"Yep. He's just your type. Got all the qualities you like."

"Which are?"

"For you, not too many muscles. Not hairy. No face fluff. Bookish. Plus extras."

I burst out laughing.

"And good looking, of course," she added. "Smart, too. In fact, he might even be as smart as you."

"So let me get this straight," I said. "What you appear to be describing is basically a geek."

"Don't forget the extras."

"Nina, I'm hanging up . . ."

"Don't you dare. Listen, I'm not kidding, Sav, he's completely perfect for you. He's—I don't know—he's really unusual. I just think . . . you'll like him."

Her breathiness caught me by surprise. It wasn't like Nina to react that way to anyone, let alone a boy. I was still suspicious, though.

"When did you meet him?"

"A few days ago."

"So he's someone from school, yeah?"

"No. You don't know him. Just get ready. And make sure you wear a dress."

"A dress?"

"Yes. A nice floral pattern. Plus a big hat. That's what he said he liked."

"You're kidding?"

"Of course I'm kidding, you idiot."

"Nina—"

"No more questions. I'll be there in an hour."

I showered, dried myself off in my bedroom, and slipped into a plain black skirt.

While I was still choosing what top to wear, Annette Coombs appeared. She's been my foster mum for the past six months. My parents were killed in a car crash when I was a baby, and I've had six or seven fosters since then. All have been nice, decent people, but I keep changing them, especially lately. It's not the fosters' fault. I just get edgy if I stay in one place too long. The constant moving around makes life a hassle for my caseworkers, but because I never cause any other problems they reluctantly put up with the drama.

Annette is already one of my all-time favorite replacement mums, though. She's warm and sensitive, and always respects my privacy. Which was why it was a surprise to see her lingering like a nervous bird outside my bedroom door.

"What is it?" I asked. "Everything OK?"

"It's . . . um, nothing really." She sounded sheepish. "It's only . . . well, I've been meaning to mention—" she shook her head. "Did you know that you're making unusual noises?"

I raised an eyebrow.

"In the middle of the night, I mean. In your sleep."

"What kind of noises?"

"Squeaks and, er . . ." She shrugged awkwardly. "Clicks."

"Clicks?" I couldn't help laughing. "You're kidding. *Clicks?*"

She shrugged. "I know, but I've been hearing them coming from your room for the past couple of weeks. At first I thought you just had a radio on low or something, but this morning one noise was so weird that I came in to check you were OK." She hesitated. "The sounds were coming *from your mouth*, Savannah. You had your lips wide open. One sound was especially odd. A sort of"—she fumbled to find the right word—"watery, liquid noise."

Crazy as all this sounded, I could tell she was being serious, so I attempted a serious answer. "My throat's been a bit sore because of my cold. Maybe my breathing's rough because of that."

"Mm." Annette didn't look convinced, and maybe she was right not to be. The truth is that my throat had been sore for ages. About a month ago, Nina got so concerned that she dragged me to my doctor, who sent me off for blood tests. I'm due to receive the results at King's Hospital tomorrow, and I can't say I'm not looking forward to it. Without understanding why, I've been feeling bizarrely protective of my throat recently. Whenever anyone questions me about the pain, I keep pretending I feel OK. Alone in bed, I've even caught myself reaching up to touch my neck. Nothing dramatic—just quiet, tender little dabs. But it's alarming because I keep finding my hand there unexpectedly. I'll raise my arm for an unrelated reason, and there my fingers will be—hovering like a shield.

And *liquid* sounds? What did that mean?

In the end, I promised Annette I'd tell the hospital about the noises when I went for my appointment tomorrow, and finished dressing. I surprised myself by being ready twenty minutes before Nina was due. I'll admit I was curious. Her enthusiasm combined with the fact that I knew nothing about this boy definitely had my interest.

Nina turned up looking as good as always, dressed in a sparkling strapless turquoise top. I smiled. It was just the sort of semi-revealing outfit bound to annoy her latest boyfriend, the pretty but none-too-bright Brent. Especially if he saw her wearing it dancing with any other boys. Nina liked annoying Brent. That and kissing him.

"You ready?" she asked, checking her watch. Nina always acts as if the whole world's keeping her waiting.

"Yep. Tell me more about this boy then."

"In a minute. Let's get going."

We jumped on the crowded 171 bus and walked up Lyndhurst Way. Nina made slow progress in her pointy killer heels. They're the highest she can wear without tipping over. Even so, they barely bring her up to five-four. Nina's always been self-conscious about her height, but recently she's filled out a little, and found a way to inject

11

a seductive swing into her hips when she puts her mind to it. My own specialty is looming over people. I'm nearly six foot, tallest girl in my class, so I'm good at that.

Walking side by side, Nina and I look odd, I suppose—mismatched, tall and short—but looks aren't everything, are they? We've known each other since we were tots. Even when I moved away a few years ago we kept in constant touch. I'd do anything for Nina, and she would for me as well.

Nina's hair looked great tonight: long swaths of vibrant auburn. My own hair is a duller brown, if you care to look up that high.

"Let's get a move on, we'll be late," she said, still offering me nothing about the mysterious boy. Typical of Nina, now she had my attention, to keep me in suspense.

"He's expecting us, is he?" I asked.

"Of course he's expecting us. I told him to get there for seven."

"Why so early?"

"I want to be sure he arrives before most of the other girls turn up. We don't want them getting in ahead of us. Damaging your chances."

I blinked at her. "What makes you think they'll be so interested in him?"

She grinned. "Intuition."

Nina had me completely hooked now, of course. Despite my misgivings about getting close to boys, I couldn't help being intrigued.

"Your throat still sounds sore," she tutted.

"Nah, it's OK." I shrugged defensively. "This cold's just dragging on, making me croaky. It's fine."

"Fine for an ax murderer, maybe."

I managed a half laugh.

"It sounds husky at least," Nina noted. "For tonight that's good. Alluring. Temptress voice. Everything helps." She smiled enigmatically. "Anyway, he's not perfect, this boy. He won't mind your croak. He's got a little defect of his own."

"Oh?"

"You'll see."

"Nina," I growled, grabbing the straps of her bag to yank her back, "you'd better tell me more about him, or I swear I'm going home right now."

"Oh . . . OK," she relented. "But I don't know much. I just found him wandering around our neighborhood last week, that's all. Lost, he was. Said he was new to the area. Just moved in and all that."

"He stopped to talk to you?"

"No. I stopped to talk to *him*, dummy. He looked lost but he also looked cute. Cute enough to really need my help."

Until now her description had all been typically brash and full-on Nina, but suddenly she looked a little . . . was that shyness I was seeing?

"So what happened?" I asked.

She shrugged as if it was nothing, but I could tell it wasn't.

"We were getting on fine," she said, when I pressed her. "You know, chatting away, blah, blah, when...well, I could tell he wasn't interested. Not in me, anyway."

I checked Nina's expression. It was oddly vulnerable. "Hey, hold on a minute," I said. "How many times have you met this boy? Be honest."

"Just that day. I was with him...no more than ten minutes."

"Ten minutes?"

"Probably less."

"He made that much of an impression on you in less than ten minutes?"

She blushed, glanced away. Circling her arm, I drew her close to me. I wasn't sure I wanted to meet this boy of hers anymore. Not if he could do this much damage so fast to someone as confident as Nina.

We walked together in silence for a few minutes, our bodies close. Eventually, Nina smiled cautiously up at me. As a little girl, I'd seen her smile that way.

"You're my best friend," she said quietly. "You know that?"

"I know." I felt emotional myself now and held her.

We finally arrived and stood outside Tori Siegler's front door a moment, neither of us knocking. Nina licked her lips and looked up at me.

"Ready?" she asked.

I blew out a long breath and rang the bell.

2

We walked into a wall of drum and bass. The usual assortment of people was lounging about on Tori's boxy sofas and chairs, and it was noisy, but at least the lamps in the room were subdued and indirect. Nina winked at me. She had a name for this kind of illumination: kissing light.

Tori was busy chatting with some boys in the kitchen, so her mum did the honors, pushing a flimsy white cardboard plate and plastic fork into my hands. "Help yourself," she said enthusiastically, waving at a food-piled table. From the look of what was there, we'd been invited to a kiddies' picnic. It was always a bit like this when you went to Tori's, but at least her mum was friendly, and it made a nice change from hanging around the dingy entrances to the Elephant and Castle shopping center. Plus she let us play our own music.

No alcohol permitted, of course. *Verboten*. Amazing how some always got smuggled in, though.

I glanced nervously around for a new face, but Nina's boy obviously hadn't turned up yet. Drearily, as I scanned the room, there wasn't a single person I didn't already know from school.

Nina handed me an orange juice from the drinks table.

"Thanks," I muttered. "What's that you've got?"

She eyed something pink and fizzy in her hand, slurping it suspiciously. "I'm not sure, but it tastes better than it looks. I don't think Mrs. Siegler realizes her little goth helper over there is spiking drinks on demand."

The goth doing the mixing was Fiona Hunter: all spiral tattoos, vampish white face powder, and smoldering eyes. She'd once pinched a boyfriend from Nina, so our rare chats were always barbed.

The bell chimed, and Mrs. Siegler headed off to the door. I tried to watch the entrance to the living room without being too obvious about it, but it turned out to be only a couple of idiot-boys Nina and I always avoided. Predictably, neither took the plate and fork Mrs. Siegler offered. While the first one mobbed Tori with his enthusiasm, the other dove straight over to the stereo to whack up the volume. He swore when someone tried to stop him, then had to apologize when he saw it was Mrs. Siegler.

Nina and I were still enjoying that when the doorbell chimed again and in wandered a new boy.

The boy?

He was slim, darkly blond, and I automatically stood up straight to get a better view of him. Primed as I was by Nina, I was expecting a vision of handsomeness, so when he wasn't quite that I had to check with her to make sure it was him. She nodded, so I turned back to assess him properly.

He was about our age and decent-looking, but not spectacularly so. True, he was tall, and he had an open, engaging face, but I couldn't see what had Nina so hot under the collar. For looks alone at least two other boys in the room had him hands down.

"Wait," Nina said, watching me closely.

"Wait for what?"

"Just wait."

Mrs. Siegler was escorting the new boy our way, laughing at some remark he'd made. I caught a few words of their exchange. He was complimenting her on the food in a way I knew she would appreciate.

"He's a charmer," I said.

Fiona Hunter detached herself like a skinny little snake from the drinks area and sidled up to me. "Like what you see?" she murmured, ignoring Nina. "He's Reece Gandolfo. Just moved to our area, apparently. Bit of a mystery boy. No one seems to know much about him, except he's some kind of athlete, training down at Battersea Park."

Nina slowly sipped her drink. "I hear he's got acute BO and mental health issues. Why don't you make your move, Fiona? He's just right for you."

Fiona smirked at her. "Where's Tom? Gone to football tonight, has he? Can't make it? Left you all alone again?"

Nina laughed, a huge unpolished guffaw. "I dumped him weeks ago. Fiona, you really need to keep up."

Half the girls in the room by now were craning their necks to get a better look at Reece Gandolfo. A few had already locked in on him like leopards waiting to graze. Intrigued, I listened in on his conversations. It didn't take me long to realize why he was attracting so much attention. There was just an easy manner about him, an understated self-assurance rare in boys our age. His voice was striking, too—not deep, but with a husky edge to it. I could see exactly why Nina had been so drawn to him.

"Want to say hello?" she murmured in my ear.

"Uh-uh," I answered. "Way too soon."

But I didn't seem to have much choice, because Tori had started introducing him to everyone. I looked about for an escape route, but that only made the boy glance in my direction. It was my first chance to get a good look at his eyes, and I'll admit they were nice: liquid brown. When he caught me checking him out, he smiled. It was a shy smile, not full of pretend confidence. I liked it.

"Hi, I'm Reece," he said, as Nina practically threw us together.

"Savannah," I said.

"Nice to meet you, Savannah."

I nodded awkwardly. From this range, I could see the little defect Nina had mentioned. Reece Gandolfo had a vivid white scar on his neck. It cut straight across his Adam's apple, and for some reason my first thought was to wonder whether or not it was self-inflicted. The scar didn't look recent, but it moved unpredictably when he talked, giving him a slight Frankenstein's-monster quality. Realizing that my gaze was being constantly drawn to it, I focused instead on his face.

"It's OK," he muttered. "I'm used to it. And by the way, just in case you're wondering, I didn't do it to myself."

"I never thought that," I said, blushing.

"You'd be amazed how many people do. It's often the first thing they assume."

"Really?" Caught out so easily, my ears glowed.

Fortunately, Tori chose that moment to whisk Reece away.

I spent the next half an hour or so chatting to various friends, but only halfheartedly. Like others at the party, my eyes kept being drawn back to Reece. Fiona obviously felt the attraction, too. She kept buzzing around him like a fly, talking practically nonstop. It was obvious he wasn't interested, though. He kept edging away from her. Not flagrantly, just enough to keep them apart. There was something familiar about the gesture as well, but I couldn't quite place it.

A few minutes later Fiona was still jabbering away in Reece's ear, getting nowhere, when Nina turned up holding a plate of sandwiches. She pressed one playfully towards Reece's lips.

His reaction shocked everyone.

Yanking his head away, he leapt back—literally jumped.

"I'm afraid I can't eat that," he announced, as if Nina had just poked a gun in his face.

All eyes in the room were instantly drawn to him. Fiona stepped away. Martyn Wright, one of the idiot-boys, sniffed. "What's the matter, mate?"

"There's nothing the matter," Reece replied. "I just can't eat anything . . . that big." The remark was so unexpected that a few people laughed. "I had an accident a number of years ago," he went on. "I can't swallow easily. My throat capacity is similar to—the width I mean—of a baby. It's easy for me to choke, that's all."

"What kind of accident?" Martyn asked.

"You don't want to know."

Martyn grinned, sharklike. "Yes, I do. Of course I do. I definitely want to know."

The two boys locked eyes. The result was interesting. I'd seen Martyn Wright stare down a few kids over the years, but not this time. Reece clearly had his measure. Gazing unwaveringly at him, the slightest of amused smiles registered around his lips as he said, "My dad did it."

That changed the atmosphere. Several people, including Martyn, looked away. Others, not quite so sure what to make of Reece Gandolfo anymore, traipsed off elsewhere. Conversations jerkily got underway again, but Reece wasn't so popular as he had been, and when Tori started serving hot snacks to guests he was left briefly near me with no one else to talk to.

"It's not a big deal," he muttered, glancing hesitantly across. "About the throat, I mean. I was only a year old when it happened. It was my birthday, actually."

"Oh?"

Reece took a breath, as if uncertain he should continue.

"It's OK," I said, smiling to give him confidence. "Go on. What happened?"

He shrugged. "I was strapped into my high chair for safety. Apparently Mum had been stuffing me with slices of ripe apple as a birthday treat. But then Dad called her about something—they could never remember after what it was—and by the time she came back I was already choking." Reece paused, rubbing his scar. "You really want to hear this?"

I nodded. I wasn't sure I wanted all the grisly details, but I didn't want to stop him, either. Reece had the look of someone who'd been trying to get his story out for a long time. I fetched us both a Coke, and we sat down together on the carpet.

"They called an ambulance," he went on, once we were settled. "But when Dad was told it was going to take at least seven or eight minutes for the ambulance to get there, he made a decision. Told Mum to get his fishing knife. Very sharp blade, apparently."

Fingering his scar again, Reece said, "Dad wasn't just being stupid. You need to understand I was suffocating at this point. Mum said my skin was practically blue. They were both sure I was going to die." He paused thoughtfully. "I've often put myself in Dad's position since. Wondered if I'd have done the same thing, given what he knew or thought he knew. Dad couldn't recall where he'd read the details of the technique he was about to attempt. But he'd read something somewhere—misread it, as it turned out."

Clearing his throat, Reece seemed concerned by how I was taking all this, but he needn't have been. Despite the gruesomeness of the tale, he definitely had my attention. I nodded for him to continue.

"OK," he said. "So Mum returns with the knife, waiting for an explanation of what Dad's going to do with it. He explained he was going to cut *below* the object stuck in my throat. A small hole in my windpipe. A little snick, just something big enough to get some air in and keep me alive, that's all. He also promised her he'd be careful." Reece hesitated. "I think that haunted him afterwards. As if he even knew how to be. Anyway, just before she died a couple of years ago, Mum told me that was the moment she placed her hand on the blade. 'Do you really think he'll die without this?' she asked him. And when Dad answered *yes*, she said, 'Then go ahead. Do what you have to. I won't blame you afterwards, no matter what happens.'"

Reece stopped speaking for a moment. His eyes were a little moist, but he wasn't embarrassed by that, and strangely, given how little we knew each other, neither was I. Instead I sat up straighter, moving closer to him.

"I've always loved Mum for telling Dad that," he said under his breath. "For having the guts to say she would forgive him no matter what happened. For having the intelligence. Knowing that despite his tough talk Dad needed to hear those words to use the knife. Anyhow, that moment passed, and then he had to put the point of the blade up against my neck, didn't he? He actually had to *do* it. According to Mum he closed his eyes, whispered some kind of prayer and made himself *push*."

"Sorry," Reece said, when I winced. "I haven't talked about this since I was a kid. I don't know why I started, really. . . ."

"No, it's OK," I said, touching his arm. "Did . . . did it work?"

Reece broke into a half laugh. "Nope, not a chance. He went in way too deep. The wrong part of my throat, too. You can imagine how much blood there was. But the really scary thing was that when Mum cleared the wound of froth Dad saw that he still hadn't made a large enough hole. I still couldn't breathe."

"He had to cut you *again*?" I said, horrified.

"He probably would have done. Luckily for me, that's when the ambulance arrived. The driver ran across, gave my stomach a gentle shove. According to Mum he only used the very tips of his fingers. And out came a wad of apple. Two minutes later they had my neck taped up and I was on my way to hospital."

Reece attempted a grin, but underneath it his face was loaded with emotion. "Anyway," he said, "they couldn't do much about . . . well . . . you know . . ." He gestured at his scar, and the look he suddenly gave me was so vulnerable that my heart went out to him.

"I don't mind the scar," I said, meaning it, and wanting him to know that. "It doesn't bother me."

"Really?" He looked genuinely surprised. Then he abruptly laughed again, a flash of white teeth, and this time his amusement seemed real. "Ah, you say that, but you haven't heard my voice when it goes wonky yet. The famous Gandolfo squeak."

"The squeak?"

"Mm. Sometimes I sound like Mickey Mouse. Or maybe Minnie. One of the Disney mice, anyway. I get mixed up between them. I'm not kidding," he said, when I gave him a doubting smile. "Once in a while my voice goes off the scale, like a choir boy hitting top C. And then sometimes there're these weird sounds as well. Little clicks. And noises way down in my throat that—"

Before he could finish, his mobile rang.

He answered and I heard urgent, garbled words down the line. It sounded like a man yelling and weeping. Reece whispered softly back, then broke the connection. Sighing heavily, he turned back to me. "This isn't good. I have to leave."

"Right now?" I said, shocked by how fast the conversation had changed.

"Yeah. Sorry. It can't wait. It . . . never mind."

Muttering a hasty good-bye to Tori, Nina, and Mrs. Siegler he headed towards the front door.

"Wait," I said—something wanting me to keep him close, not let him get away. "Can I . . . can I call you?" I held my breath, excruciatingly embarrassed.

He licked his lips, nearly said something, then stopped.

"I mean," I said, "if you want me to, that is. . . ." I blushed as my words dried up.

But Reece looked pleased. "Yeah," he said. "That would be good." A broad smile spread across his face. "I'd really like that."

So we exchanged mobile numbers and, feeling a sense of euphoria I couldn't quite explain, I hovered near the back door, waiting for him to go. Nina gave me a big I-told-you-so smile, and together we watched as Reece Gandolfo buttoned up his grey leather jacket, adjusted his collar, and headed off into the chill of the night.

By the time I got my head out of its daze the party was starting to wind down in a series of slow-edged pop numbers. Nina, looking tired from dancing, joined me by the fire. She slumped against my arm, wiping a smudge of mascara from her cheek.

"Stay still," I said, wetting my finger to clean it off.

When I was done she crossed her eyes. "How do I look now?"

"Perfect," I said. "Brent never made it, huh?"

"Nope. He's unreliable." She laughed. "I'd dump him if he wasn't such a good kisser."

"Does that matter so much?" I asked, the question having more meaning tonight than usual.

"It does when you're kissing someone."

Martyn Wright appeared from a side room, looking bleary-eyed, and surprised and disappointed to still find us here. Nina glared at him.

"That Reece," she said. "His eyes were all over you. He wasn't interested in anyone else. Fiona didn't even get a look in. You saw that, didn't you?"

"I'm not sure what I think of him yet," I murmured.

Nina massaged her toes and slid a little closer, wriggling her nose. "I reckon it would be dead easy to fall for a boy like him."

"Maybe," I said. But I wasn't so sure. Nina was always falling for boys, but I'd never felt the kind of romantic love she meant.

We sat together for a few minutes, not saying anything. From the dance floor a boy exited, alone, and somewhere behind us Tori started turning the lights up a notch—all that moody kissing light fading away.

Tightening the straps of her shoes, Nina gave Martyn one last withering look. "C'mon, Sav, no talent left," she muttered. "Let's get out of here."

3

Many hours later, long after Savannah Grey had put to sleep all thoughts of Reece Gandolfo, a shy moon came out from behind mounting clouds. Later still a wind arose, showering leaves across the bleak square blocks of the council estate where she lived. So many leaves were there that even the Horror—slinking between buildings—lifted its single eye to the heavens and wondered.

But it soon forgot the leaves. The prospect of hurting Savannah Grey was far more interesting.

Slipping through an open window, the Horror scampered straight up to her bedroom this time, leaning its pinched, hungry face across her pillow. Its task was merely to report on the noises from her throat again, but that was dull work. When could it kill her? The execution order was bound to arrive soon, it consoled itself. Perhaps, if it was lucky, it would be ordered to perform the execution of Savannah Grey alone. More likely it would be joined by the larger Nyktomorph. Two monsters, after all, were better than one.

Or perhaps—was it possible?—the ancient Ocrassa might undertake the killing itself. The Horror sucked in an eager breath at the possibility of that. The Ocrassa had the blood of every type of creature in the world on its hands. On its feet as well, and any number of its mouths. It lived to hunt, but the one thing it had lacked for millennia on this planet was a satisfactory opponent.

Was Savannah worthy enough?

Not yet, the Horror decided. Not unless she developed fast. It hoped she would. What was the point of an easy kill?

Tomorrow we'll do it, the Horror thought in its own language, chanting the words over and over like the child it was. *Tomorrow or the next day*. And patting its heavy jaw, it sprang from the room.

But it couldn't resist returning one last time. Bowing towards the bed, it raised its star-face high. And then, as if it wanted to astound Savannah, even now to amaze her, the Horror ran to the front of the house and with a casual flourish—*phht*—yanked the door crisply shut with its tongue.

Outside, the Nyktomorph waited. If there was any uncertainty about the Horror being a true monster there could be no doubt about this creature. The Nyktomorph was huge. Its eyes alone were the width of the Horror's entire head. Despite all this, it was camouflaged so flawlessly that, even against the straight lines of the buildings, it could not be seen.

The Horror bounded across Savannah's garden, to be greeted by the Nyktomorph's kisses. The Nyktomorph swept the Horror up in its claws, pressing it fervently against its vast chest. Then it dimmed its skin, blended into the darkness—and leapt.

A man coming home late from work saw it—or thought he did. Saw something, anyway. A blur. A shadow. No more than that. A colossal half-shape that drew leaves restlessly after it. And then the Nyktomorph and the Horror faded like a dream into the night.

4

The next morning, my mind was still filled with tantalizing thoughts about Reece Gandolfo, but I didn't have time to dwell on them. I had my 9:30 throat appointment at King's Hospital.

Nina came with me, and I was glad of her company. Without knowing why, all night I'd been worried about the prospect of someone digging around inside my mouth.

We were met at the hospital outpatient reception desk by a dapper middle-aged man with a prim yellow tie. He introduced himself as "Professor Oliver Wicken, Head of Medicine at King's Hospital." Nina suppressed a giggle at the tie, but I was more interested in why someone so important was taking a personal interest in my throat. Professor Wicken (or *Olly* as he encouraged me to call him, he definitely wanted to be on first name terms, which only made me more nervous) ushered us into his big office and sat us down.

"And how are you feeling?" he asked me, after a few administrative preliminaries.

I was tempted to lie, but Olly had an impressive air of authority about him which made it hard.

"I'm . . . er, OK," I mumbled. "Bit of a cold, that's all."

"Her throat's bad," Nina said. "It's been sore for ages. Come on, Sav, confess."

"She's exaggerating," I told him. "It's just tender. I'm taking painkillers for it. They work."

"Do they now?" Olly raised an eyebrow, obviously able to see straight through me. He tapped the desk with his slim fingers. "Have you been suffering headaches? Or had a fever? Night sweats? Anything like that?"

"No," I said truthfully, wondering where all this was leading. Olly leaned keenly forward, his hands folded across the desk. "How about pain when you swallow?"

"Uh . . . yes," I admitted, a ripple of unease shooting down my spine. "A bit of trouble when I eat."

"I didn't know that," Nina said in surprise.

I shrugged, embarrassed. I hadn't wanted to draw attention to my neck, that's all.

"Well," Olly said, "the pain's no real surprise to us, given the activity we've detected in your thyroid."

"My thyroid?" Something about the way he said it made me squeeze Nina's hand.

31

"It's a small throat gland that controls your metabolism," he explained. "We're getting decidedly odd readings from it. In particular, we're seeing the presence of *growth hormones.* That's not unusual in someone your age, but the volume is. One of my team wants to get a closer look at you."

A woman entered the room. Crisp white coat. Very competent-looking in a stern kind of way.

"This is Carol Edilman," Olly announced. "She's a specialist in ear, nose, and throat disorders. What we call an ENT."

"Hi," Carol said briskly, checking her notes. "Savannah, isn't it? I'd like to have a quick look inside your mouth, if I may?"

The request sounded reasonable enough, but my body instantly started sending warning signals.

"Don't worry," Carol reassured me, seeing me tense up. "The examination won't hurt. All I do is hold your tongue down with this"—she waved a wooden implement the size of a popsicle stick at me—"and shine my little torch." She smiled.

"No," I heard myself say. "No. I . . . I don't want you to do that."

Olly studied me thoughtfully. "Has anyone examined your throat before? I mean properly, for abnormalities or obstructions?"

"No." My voice sounded edgy. I tried to keep it under control, not understanding why I was reacting this way.

"I'm fine," I said. "Honestly, no one needs to look at me. I don't want you to. I don't want anyone . . . probing inside there."

"Sav?" Nina whispered from the side of her mouth. "What are you doing?"

"I won't touch your throat itself," Carol promised. "You don't have to swallow anything, if that's what concerns you. It's—"

"No," I said. "No." A hot flush suddenly ran through me. "Stay away. Keep back. Don't come anywhere near me."

Don't come anywhere near me? Where had that come from? Olly and Carol Edilman weren't any nearer to me than before. I couldn't believe what I did next, either. I backed away. Stepping across the room, I put half the floor between me and everyone else.

Nina, shocked, said, "Sav, they're only trying to help."

I swallowed. I had no idea why I was retreating. All I knew was that I didn't want anyone tinkering with my neck.

"Let's try a compromise here," Olly said smoothly, keeping his voice light to defuse the atmosphere. "Carol, can you maintain a certain distance from Savannah's mouth while you do your checks?"

"Yes, I suppose," she muttered. "It won't be easy, but . . ." She shrugged.

After a moment's hesitation I agreed to that and sat down again. Carol, glancing apprehensively at Olly the whole time, approached me. When she was an arm's length away she flicked her torch on and peered down at me expectantly. The situation was so absurd that she stifled a giggle.

"Uh . . . you need to open your mouth," she said.

"How wide?" I asked, deadly serious.

"As wide as possible."

I tried—but found I could barely open my lips.

I gave Nina a horrified look.

What was wrong with me? Why was I so scared of people getting near my throat?

Olly leaned back in his chair, clearly fascinated by my behavior. Carol waited, torch poised. Nina just looked worried. Sweeping past the others, she said, "Sav, you want to get out of here? You wanna go?"

"No, I'm . . . I'm OK," I managed, giving her a tight smile. "Let them do it. I know it's important for them to check."

Nina went back to her seat, and I parted my lips. It was impossible to open them far, but Carol took her chance, quickly flicking her torch around, concentrating on the depths of my throat. She didn't say anything until the examination was complete, and when she did speak it was to Olly, not me.

"It's not a problem with the tonsils," she noted. "There are some kind of . . . honey-colored, striped bands coating the inside of her throat. And I can see dark mounds lower down, either side of the larynx."

"Constricting her throat?" Olly asked sharply.

"No, I don't think so. At first I thought they were nod-
ules on the vocal cords, which isn't uncommon, but it's
not that. I've never seen anything like this before."

Honey-colored stripes? Dark mounds? What was she talking about? I had to know. Wiping a trickle of sweat from
my forehead, I took a couple of steadying breaths. "Look
again, but please hurry," I whispered, inviting her forward. "I'm not faking this. For some reason I can't keep
my mouth open for long."

Carol nodded, angling her torch down my neck. Then
she did something I realized afterwards she must have
done a thousand times. Out of pure habit, I'm certain,
she reached into the lower right pocket of her jacket for
the thin wooden spatula she used to hold down a patient's
tongue—and prodded it into my mouth.

As soon as the spatula crossed the plane of my lips my
body did two things over which I had no control. First
I stood, the swiftness of the motion sending my chair
crashing against the wall behind. Second, one of my arms
shot forward. In a blur of speed, my clenched hand took
the shortest possible route to Carol's head and *struck out*.

It all happened unbelievably fast, and when I hit her it was
so hard that I think the only reason every bone in her face
wasn't shattered was that she managed to turn her cheek
aside at the last second. Even so, the sheer unexpectedness
of the attack made everyone gasp, including me.

"Sav, what are you doing?" Nina breathed. I gazed in
disbelief at Carol. She was kneeling down, clutching her

chin in agony. "I'm . . . so sorry," I said. "Oh God . . ." I burst into bewildered tears. "I didn't mean—oh, I'm so sorry. . . ."

Olly helped Carol up, but stared at me. "You didn't mean to do that, did you? It was . . . an involuntary reflex of your arm."

For a moment I stared in dismay at Carol. Then I glanced at the arm which had struck out. I held my hand up, sensing the power there, the further damage it could easily have done. I should stay, I thought. Make sure Carol's OK. But I was suddenly too frightened by the closeness of the bodies around me to stay in the building. I had to get out.

5

I ran. I shot so fast from the hospital that even Nina, scrambling after me, yelling my name, couldn't keep up. Only the heavy traffic on the high street slowed me down.

Squeezing into an alleyway between two shops, I tearfully tried to get my mind under some kind of control.

What's happening to my throat? I thought, my breath coming out in terrified gasps. *Why am I so scared?*

Camberwell's roads were crowded with people. Feeling a desperate need to be alone, I left the alley and ran on, driven by the necessity to get away from everyone, to find somewhere safe.

But where was safe?

Anywhere they can't get at your throat, came the understanding.

"Sav, where're you going?" Nina cried, finally catching up with me outside Nando's restaurant.

"Stay back," I yelled, my whole body recoiling like a frightened animal.

She stopped in the middle of the pavement, staring up in astonishment. "Sav, you're not scared of *me*, are you?"

Thinking of what I'd done to Carol, I could only burst into tears. I didn't know what had happened in Olly's office, but I couldn't risk Nina getting hurt as well.

"OK, we're going to my place. Right now." Nina thrust her arm in mine, giving me no chance to wriggle out of it. "No arguing. Come on."

She held me tightly until we reached her house, practically dragging me up to her second-floor bedroom.

As soon as I was inside, I disentangled our arms. Before I did anything else I had to know what Carol Edilman had seen. Striding across the room to a large mirror on the far wall, I tried opening my mouth—only to find that again there was resistance. Even here—safe at Nina's—I could barely part my lips.

Fear shrieking through me, I tried prying my jaw wide with both hands.

With a distinct *slap*, one hand knocked the other down.

When that happened I couldn't stop my body running hot and cold with panic. Nina reacted the same way, letting out a little scream behind me, and for several seconds I simply stared at my own pale reflection in the mirror. Then a thought jumped into my mind. I'd woken this morning from a nightmare about a monster. I'd been having the same harrowing dream almost every day for months. In the dream I never saw the monster itself—it was in a wood, obscured by leaves—but I was forever hunting it. And though I wasn't sure what made me think about that now, as I turned towards Nina I whispered my fear. I said it out loud. I uttered the word *monster.*

And my throat . . . reacted. As soon as the second syllable left my tongue, something detached itself and flowed from deep inside my throat.

A sound.

A dreamily quiet bubble of noise.

Nina stared openmouthed at me as it gushed inside my throat, sweeping ticklishly upward. For a moment the bubble seemed to teeter, pausing uncertainly on the tip of my tongue. Then it fell with a pure musical *pop* into the space between us.

"Sav?" Nina murmured. But before I could even think about answering her a new group of sounds were flooding towards my lips. These ones were even purer in tone than the first. Tripping out in clusters of twos and threes, initially they seemed random, with no discernable pattern. But I soon realized that what I was hearing was a sequence—*a scale of musical notes.*

Each note was a perfect, natural octave above the next.

The sounds kept coming. I couldn't hold them back. Every time I shut my mouth my lips flew wide again, and next thing I knew, a set of dazzling flats and sharps were zipping past my molars. They were followed by a group of high-pitched *pips*, each running up and down the entire frequency sound range in what seemed like a controlled progression.

I stood there, covering my mouth with my hands, but no matter what I did I couldn't hold the noises in. Trills shot out. Clashing vibrations. Shimmers. Chimes. And both Nina and I gave a yelp of fear when a final noise emerged. This one wasn't musical. It was as dark and heavy as brass. Rooted at the base of my throat, it boomed out explosively inside my neck, my eyes snapping wide open as it emerged in a crackle of menacing *clicks* that sizzled past my tongue.

And then it was over.

Over instantly.

As abruptly as they had started, the noises came to a halt.

For a while, Nina and I just stood in terrified silence, holding our breaths, but no more sounds emerged. The musical performance was over. *Shut down*, I couldn't help thinking. *As if my throat's been through a test, and now that test is complete.*

The last sound, the *clicks*, gradually receded, but for several seconds afterwards I could still feel their echoes firing at intervals inside my neck. Normal background noises—garden birds, next door's lawnmower—replaced them, spectacularly bland after what had come before.

Across the room, Nina was holding her hands to her face.

"Sav, you . . . you've got to go back to the hospital," she rasped. She reached out to pull me close, but backed off when another *click* burst from my mouth. "Oh, Sav . . . Oh God, what's happening to you?"

We were both crying, and I wanted desperately to hug Nina, but I didn't dare risk getting so close.

Then my mobile rang. It was Annette. Olly had called her. Apparently I'd broken Carol Edilman's jaw, but Olly wanted to reassure me that I wouldn't be prosecuted for it. He just wanted me to come in for a fuller examination. How could I, though? The news about Carol only confirmed how dangerous it was for me to be near people.

I muttered a few vague reassurances to Annette, then ended the call—and backed further away from Nina.

"You wouldn't hurt me," she murmured. "Sav, you wouldn't do that."

"Wouldn't I? How do you know?" I said, keeping my distance. "I attacked that ENT doctor, didn't I? As soon as she stuck that spatula thing inside my lips, my arm went for her. If she'd gone further down—"

"You think you might have done something worse?"

"I'm not sure. Maybe."

"Listen to me," Nina whispered, seeing me shiver. "You've got to go straight back to the hospital and get whatever that *thing* is taken out of your throat. Do it right now. Stop mucking about. Come on. . . ."

She went to grab my arm, but I wouldn't let her.

"I . . . I don't think it's harming me," I said.

"What? What are you talking about? How can you know that?"

She was right. How could I possibly know? But as a look of disbelief creased Nina's face, somehow, frighteningly, I did. Whatever was in my throat, at some instinctive level I sensed that I needed it. In fact, with a baffled sense of wonder, I realized that far from being harmful to me, it felt more like it was there . . . to *protect* me.

And no sooner had I thought that than my mind flew back to Reece Gandolfo's words at the party. Hadn't he talked about odd noises from his throat as well? Clicks? Booming sounds?

With Nina watching me closely, I tapped the number he'd given me into my mobile. Reece took his time answering, and when he finally came on the line I didn't tell him why I was phoning. It just felt too crazy to blurt out over the phone. But he must have caught the fear in my voice because he immediately gave me his address and said, "Come over this afternoon, after lunch."

"Not now?" I pressed.

"No, I'm sorry but you can't. My dad's gone missing, and I've got to find him. He does this sometimes, and he'll be upset afterwards, need calming down. I'll explain everything when I see you later."

I decided to wait in Nina's bedroom until it was time to see Reece. It felt safer here than outside, and in any case I was too scared to go out. Nina kept arguing with me about going back to the hospital, but I resisted her. I just knew I should stay away from people for now. I couldn't take the risk of allowing anyone near my throat.

It was maybe half an hour later that Nina—gasping, pointing from her window—noticed what was going on outside the house. The entire neighborhood was inundated with leaves. They were everywhere. In the sky. Drifting against gates. Blanketing rooftops. Filling gutters.

"What is it?" she wondered. "Some kind of freak storm?"

But it didn't look like that to me. It was a breezy autumn day, but there was nowhere near enough wind to account for this number of leaves. And maybe the wind itself was distracting me, or it was some weird trick of the light, but just for a second, as I stared, my eyes seemed to fast-flicker as well, and I could have sworn that I saw movement—*a pattern in the motion of the leaves.*

The moment passed, leaving me only with an ominous feeling I couldn't quite hold on to. Nina gazed fearfully at me, then turned back to look outside again.

We watched for the next hour as more leaves gathered around her house. I'd never seen so many varieties. Sycamore and oak. Ash and birch. Dense patches of hawthorn. And suddenly my mind raced back to the monster nightmares. In those, wasn't the creature always surrounded by leaves? What did that mean? *That it was close? That it was nearby?* But it wasn't real, was it? It was only a dream. Until this moment, I'd never seriously considered that a true monster was out there, waiting for me, but was it possible? Something huge and ancient, concealed by leaves? I couldn't shake that terrifying thought from my mind.

And why did I get the unnerving feeling that I was meant to go out into the world to find it?

6

The Ocrassa monster arrived from space on a puff of solar wind at the dawn of life on our world. It was infinitesimal—a tiny seedling within a dry, tough husk.

Unheralded, the deadly seedling landed in a cloud and automatically tested the atmosphere. Registering the presence of heavy elements like carbon, it sank lower.

Where there was carbon, there was life.

Life meant food.

The seedling had wandered the universe for millions of years, waiting for this moment. Its species always spread this way. Evolutionarily, given the vast emptiness between stars, there was no other way to travel between the worlds except on the delicate breath of solar energy.

Time to open.

A trickle of enzymes cracked the husk, and the Ocrassa blew seven times around our planet's windy skies before landing.

It settled on an outcrop of bare rock.

On the rock it waited, without any comprehension of what it waited for. Earth was a forbidding planet. Cold. Devoid at this early stage of all except the smallest single-celled organisms. Food was scarce, and would be for another three billion years. Never again in its long life would the Ocrassa be so vulnerable—a diminutive atom, pitched against nature's vastness.

But the Ocrassa did not shiver. In its own way, it was the perfect blueprint: an organism designed to adapt to any new world.

Its first task was to survive. For eons it was incessantly lashed by acid rain, and it should have perished, but it endured. It endured because real monsters are hard to kill, and this monster was especially difficult to kill, the hardest of all.

And finally another life-form—a microscopic amoeba—bumped idly against it.

The Ocrassa reacted at once.

Instinct is faster than thought.

It lunged—invading the living tissue of the amoeba. With shocking speed, the Ocrassa punctured the amoeba's skin and wriggled inside. Then, squirming towards the nucleus—the brain—it took control.

And now there were new possibilities.

Now it had a real body.

Now it could move, could hunt.

Instantly, the Ocrassa unhooked its secure perch on the rock and let its new form drift inside a watery pool. In time another single-celled organism collided with it. Reacting fast, the Ocrassa sliced open the organism's membrane and sucked it dry.

The Ocrassa did not know it was feeding. It did not even understand that it was killing another living creature. Concepts of life and death meant nothing to it yet. But after absorbing the organism the Ocrassa later felt an absence of something. It noted hunger. And once it knew that, it would never be satisfied.

It would always be hungry.

7

Reece lived on Cadiz Street, not far from me. Reaching the end of the street just after lunch, Nina and I found him standing on the footpath. His back was to us, his arm supporting a much older, barefooted man dressed only in a black bathrobe.

It had to be Reece's dad, but it was shocking to see how ill he looked. He could only shuffle down the path. At one point he twisted around, furiously arguing. Reece didn't argue back, just waited for him to run out of breath, then gently guided him forward again.

"Let me do this alone," I said to Nina, after Reece had reached his house and shut the door.

"No way you're keeping me out of there," Nina told me.

"Nina, please. If you're near me, I'll just be worried all the time. Let me see him on my own first." She argued, swearing a couple of times, but eventually agreed to stay back at her house.

After she'd gone, and I'd waited a decent interval for Reece to settle his dad, I knocked timidly on their front door. Getting no answer, I glanced through the open window of the living room. Inside, the grey-haired Mr. Gandolfo was slumped on a low wooden chair, his bathrobe sagging over his knees. He looked completely exhausted.

Not wanting to startle him, I tapped the window as lightly as I could. He stirred at the sound, but didn't see me. Watery blue eyes peered only vaguely in my general direction.

Mr. Gandolfo's resemblance to Reece was obvious, but he was ravaged by illness. His skin was purpled with veins, his whole face crisscrossed with the sort of detailed lines you normally associate with the elderly, not someone who, judging from his body shape, was still only late middle-aged. The whole right side of his cheek was lopsided as well, tilted downward at the mouth. A stroke?

There was no sign of Reece, though I could hear rummaging activity upstairs.

I was still feeling like an intruder, and wondering how to introduce myself through the window, when his dad spotted me.

"Hi, I'm . . . I'm so sorry to bother you," I said. "I'm a friend of Reece's. I met him at a party last night."

Mr. Gandolfo's eyes narrowed as he rose from his seat. A tremor rippled through his right arm, confirming my suspicion about a stroke.

"No, please don't get up," I said, suddenly realizing he might be overexerting himself.

Not listening, Mr. Gandolfo heaved himself upright. His knuckles were white with effort. Swaying, he took a single baby step towards the window, then lost his balance, crashing forward.

"Stay still!" I told him. "Wait for Reece. He can't be far..."

But Mr. Gandolfo hauled himself upright, his bleary eyes seeking mine. When he found me again his lips worked frighteningly hard to form words, but only groans came out. Frustrated, he swiveled his body around to the staircase behind him.

Halfway up that staircase, his face part in shadow, stood Reece.

In his hands were several bandages and what looked like disinfectant. "Dad, no, don't move," he sighed. "Stay where you are."

I suddenly saw red smears on the floor, and realized with horror that Mr. Gandolfo's bare feet were trailing blood.

Reece rushed down the stairs, still showing no sign of having seen me. Approaching his dad with the utmost gentleness, he folded his dad's palsied hand against his side. "It's OK," he said, delicately massaging his dad's fingers, as if using touch to remind him who he was. Then, guiding him back to the wooden chair, Reece dipped a towel in a strong-smelling antiseptic solution and began bathing his feet.

I hovered outside the window, a silent witness. I was mesmerized by the care Reece took, the meticulous way he cleaned, wrapped and then double-wrapped bandages around the wounds.

"What's wrong?" Reece asked, following his dad's eyes. That led him to my face at the window.

"Oh," he gasped. "It's you!"

"I'm sorry," I said, embarrassed. "I knocked first. I tried to explain through the window, but your dad . . ." I gestured to show he couldn't answer.

Mr. Gandolfo continued to mouth formless words at me. There were tears of effort in his eyes. There were tears in Reece's eyes as well.

"He's only trying to say hello," Reece explained. "He's thanking you for coming, aren't you, Dad? He just wants to do that."

"This is a bad time for you," I said, getting ready to leave. "I'll come back later, when you're finished."

"No, hold on, don't go," Reece said quickly. He finished bandaging his dad's feet, then gathered up the spare dressings and opened the front door to let me in. "Just wait in my room. It's upstairs, first on the right." Twisting around again, he murmured, "It's OK, Dad. This is Savannah. The girl I met at the party. I told you about her, remember?"

When the words went unacknowledged, Reece gestured sadly at me. "Sorry, just give me a few minutes. . . ."

I made my way up the staircase. Reece's room was untidy: the bed unmade, clothes flung everywhere. But above a pine bookcase, in neat contrast, dozens of carefully arranged photos of Reece and his parents lined the walls. I was touched by how many there were, but dismayed as well to see how recently Mr. Gandolfo had been a much healthier, vibrant-looking man. I was still studying the photos, searching for pictures of Reece as a younger boy, and any brothers and sisters he might have, when footsteps sounded on the stairs. Not wanting to appear as if I'd been snooping around, I quickly removed a pair of briefs from the only chair in the room and sat on it.

"Dad's fine," Reece whispered from the door. "I just needed to make sure he knew I'd be up here with you. It takes him a while to understand these days. It's—" he smiled self-consciously—"it's good to see you." Sitting down on the edge of his bed, he grimaced at the room's mess.

"It's OK," I told him. "Way better than mine."

Realizing that I wasn't quite ready to tell him why I was here yet, I looked around, picking a photo at random from the wall. It showed an attractive older woman with her arm around Reece's shoulder.

"Your mum?" I asked softly.

"Yeah." Reece said it with obvious pride.

"She was lovely."

"Yes, she was. Right to the end."

I glanced around the walls. Images of his parents were everywhere, but none of anyone else. "Any brothers or sisters?" I asked.

"No."

It was a definite no, but as he looked up I saw a surge of emotion, as if maybe there *had* been. A dead brother or sister? For a second Reece looked as if he was about to blurt something. Then he shook his head, and I decided that if it was anything important he'd tell me in his own time.

Downstairs there were grunts, and Reece briefly went back to the kitchen to deal with his dad. "It's not easy seeing him like this, is it?" he said, when he returned. "Dad still wants to say hello to people, welcome them in. Trouble is, he can't anymore. He keeps getting stuck and having to start over."

After a pause, I asked, "What happened to him?"

"It was a stroke. Three big ones, actually, after Mum died two years ago. They all came in a row, and now he's got complications. He can still look after himself in a basic way, but he loses it occasionally. We get nurses in here twice a day, and home help as well, so we're fine, only... he'll hate it that you came across him like this, not at his best."

"Reece, I'm ... so sorry it's like this for you," I said, knowing how inadequate those words sounded.

"Hey, it's OK. It's just that sometimes, if no one's in the house with him, Dad . . . well, tends to go wandering off."

"I saw the blood on his feet."

"Believe it or not, he's looking for Mum." Reece shook his head. "He sometimes forgets she's not with us anymore. Taking his shoes off is a more recent thing. It doesn't matter how many times you tell him not to, he still does it. Why's there so much damn glass around here, anyway?"

"I think he wanted to tell me something," I said.

"It was just his way of welcoming you, Savannah."

"Are you sure? It seemed really important to him."

Reece sighed. "I know how it looks, but Dad talks practically nonstop to anyone who comes near the house. He's always dragging strangers in. It's part of his condition, I think. Once in a while he makes sense, but mostly it's just garbled."

Reece stayed silent a moment. Then, taking an uncertain breath, he said, "I have to admit I didn't expect to see you again."

"Why?" I asked, taken aback.

"Oh, you know, starting off by telling that gruesome throat story at the party. And, well—" he fingered his scar—"this doesn't always make it easy for people, whatever they might say the first time you meet them."

"I meant what I said about the scar," I told him. And then, since he was inviting honesty, I decided to come clean about why I was here. "Reece, there's—" how was I supposed to say this without freaking him out?—"there's something in my throat."

His eyes widened. "Go on."

"I don't know what it is, but for some reason I've been feeling . . . *protective* of it. I can't even let people near my mouth."

I told him everything: the fiasco with Henry Duke, the throat noises, attacking the doctor, the honey-colored stripes, the dark bulges. By the time I finished I half-expected to see a look of incomprehension on Reece's face—maybe even a grimace of disgust—but instead his expression was full of cautious excitement. And when I mentioned the clicks, he sat up abruptly.

"Does it feel like you want to take care of what's inside?" he said in a hushed tone. "To guard whatever's in there? Shield it?"

I sat there, stunned. "You . . . you've got the same thing?"

He nodded.

"What is it?" I whispered. "What on earth is it?"

"I don't know," he whispered back. "But it's important. We both know that, don't we?" He breathed out heavily, his eyes drinking me in. "I can't believe we're having this conversation," he said, his head bent in relief. "I thought it was just me. I've been alone with this for months. Scared as hell. Like you, not able to get close to people. Thinking I was the only one. But—"

"There are two of us," I murmured. A moment of rapt silence followed, when all we did was stare at each other.

Then I said, "But it can't just be us, can it? I mean, if we're like this surely there have to be others."

If the two of us were affected, why not more people? Why not *hundreds* more? But somehow I knew that wasn't the case, and from Reece's expression he obviously felt the same way.

"Just me and you, then," he said under his breath.

"Maybe it's some kind of growth," I suggested. "It hurts enough. Cancer, maybe. Or a tumor. Something grisly like that."

"Something bad, you mean? Something to be afraid of?" Reece shook his head. "I wondered about that, too, but now that I've met you I don't think so. If it was bad, why would we both want to protect it so much?"

He shuffled back on his bed, suddenly looking uncomfortable. "Listen," he muttered, "I need to summon up a bit of courage here. I'm afraid I've got a confession to make. I don't think you're going to like it."

"Oh?" It was such an abrupt change in direction that my heart missed a beat.

"I wasn't totally honest with you last night at the party," Reece said. "Actually, I wasn't honest at all. I'd seen you before. The truth is that I've been thinking about you for a long time, Savannah Grey."

8

"There's only one way to do this," Reece said tentatively, sucking in his lower lip. "I'm just going to tell you everything in one go and take the consequences. Is that OK?"

I wasn't sure what he expected me to say to that. I just nodded.

"All right. Here goes. To start with it wasn't at Tori's party that I first saw you. It was about eight weeks before that. I knew something extraordinary was going on, though, because the moment I spotted you I felt, well, *incredible*." Reece took a couple of steadying breaths. "It was a Tuesday evening, raining, and you were kind of hunched over, keeping dry in a shop doorway. I bet you can't remember what you were wearing that day, but I can. It was a dark brown suede jacket with a hood that didn't quite cover your bangs."

Reece didn't wait for me to react to that, just continued.

"Your hair at the front was already so soaked that it was flat against your head, like this." He flattened his own hair, and I half laughed, as much out of nervousness as anything else. "Anyway, you left the doorway and started running. That gave me a choice: either forget about you and stay dry, or follow you out into the rain. I decided to follow you. Don't ask me why. I just had to. But of course I didn't have an umbrella, did I? So there I was, slipping up every few strides, following behind you like some kind of creepy guy, getting even wetter than you were.

"And I was lost as well." Reece shook his head ruefully. "Me and Dad had just moved to this area. I didn't have a clue where I was. Anyhow, you ran—and by the way do you know how fast you run, Savannah?—until finally you stopped outside your house." Reece smirked. "You took forever searching for your keys. I thought you'd never find the damned things. I should have said hello, but I decided you'd think I was some kind of nutter, running up to you all soaked like that. You swore. Twice, actually, before you found the keys. Until Tori's party those were the only words I'd ever heard you say." He eyed me warily. "I'm freaking you out with all this, aren't I?"

"A bit," I said. But in truth he wasn't. There *was* something between us after all. Suddenly noticing how close I'd been leaning towards him, I drew back. I didn't want to risk a repeat of what had happened to the doctor. But then I thought: if there's such a strong connection between us, isn't it safe to get closer? I was tempted to try straight away—to touch him—but held back.

"The moment I saw you that first day I knew we were supposed to meet," Reece went on. "But then I did something dumb. I forgot to note your address." He laughed. "I was feeling so happy I just walked away in a daze. And afterwards, no matter how hard I tried, I couldn't find your house again. I didn't know the area. The streets, the houses, all looked the same to me. . . ."

He sat back on his bed, an awed expression on his face.

"I thought that was it, that I'd never see you again. But then I met Nina after a training run at Battersea Park. I was lost, and we got chatting. She invited me to Tori's party, and, well . . . there you were."

I swallowed. I was embarrassed to be the focus of so much absorbed attention, but I found myself wanting Reece to go on.

"Why didn't you tell me all this at the party?"

"I meant to," he said. "I should have. But when I rehearsed it in my mind it sounded too weird to come straight out with. And then, after the embarrassing stuff with the sandwich, I guess I lost my nerve. But at least I got a chance to watch you. I couldn't help noticing the way you kept your face away from people. Especially your mouth." He narrowed his eyes. "We're alike that way, Savannah. And based on what you've told me about your throat, I'm wondering if we're alike in other ways, too."

I felt myself stiffen, having no idea where he was going with this. "What ways?"

"OK, where should we start? School, maybe. I get pretty good grades. Especially in sciences. And I like maths. Particularly geometry." Seeing my expression, he smiled. "You really like geometry as well, eh?"

I couldn't take my eyes off Reece.

"You've moved around a lot as well, haven't you?" he said. "Changed your home address every few years. Only it wasn't your parents who wanted to move?"

"I get restless," I whispered, explaining about my fosters.

"Me, too. Dad didn't want to leave the last place to come here. It was me who forced his hand."

My mouth felt dry, and I ran my tongue over my lips. "Why do you think we do that? You think we're afraid of something?"

"Afraid?"

"Of being tracked? Of being found. *Of getting caught.*"

I let that unnerving possibility hang in the air between us a moment. Then, when I mentioned the monster dreams I'd been having, Reece glanced up.

"Yeah, I've had those dreams," he murmured shakily. "The monster in the wood. Shared dreams," he mused. "You don't really think there's a monster out there waiting for us, do you? You don't actually believe it's real?"

When I nodded he swallowed. Then he sat up, an excited edge cutting through his voice. "Then . . . is that why we've met? Is that why you're here? Have we been brought together to fight the *same* monster?"

I sat there reeling for a moment, trying to take that in. "But even if that's true, why us?"

"Why not us?" he answered bleakly. "Why should it have to be someone else?" His eyes shone, never leaving mine. "You know, I've been having that dream for ages. And every time I have it the creature always feels too big for me to handle on my own. But if you're right—if there really is something out there—at least we're not alone. We can face it together."

He said those words with such straightforward conviction that I couldn't help myself. I stretched out to touch his cheek. In that moment it seemed the most natural thing in the world to do. But before my hand reached him, I stopped. A trickle of cold sweat was running down my back.

"What's wrong?" Reece asked.

"I . . . I don't know."

He looked crestfallen, but not surprised. "You're scared of me, aren't you? You're scared to get anywhere near me."

"It's not that," I lied, devastated by my own reaction.

"You are. You pulled back. You flinched. I saw you."

"Reece, I'm sorry. I . . . I don't know why I did that." But my mind was screaming at me, *Can't I even get near Reece? Can't I even do that? Please, I have to be able to do that. Don't separate me from him as well as everyone else.*

He looked as crushed as me. "I'm the same, Savannah. Exactly the same. I thought—hoped—with you . . . never mind. Not one inch closer than we already are, eh?"

He lay grimly back on his bed, looking defeated, and for a few minutes we both just sat there, our eyes averted, and all I could think was, *How can we fight a monster together if we can't even get close to each other?*

Then he pushed himself up on the bed and faced me squarely. "Can I ask you a really odd question? It's sort of personal."

I nodded.

"OK, don't misunderstand me, I can see you're close to Nina, but have you ever felt really close to anyone else?"

"What do you mean by close?"

"I mean emotionally. You know, real friendships. Unbreakable bonds. People you can't live without, that kind of thing."

I looked directly at Reece, trying to read his expression. He wasn't playing games with me. It was a genuine question. And the answer over a lifetime had to be *yes*. But, of course, when I really thought about the way I'd always moved from place to place, it wasn't.

"Nor me," Reece said softly. "We're not too sure about getting close to anyone, are we? Especially someone new. And especially *physically*." He sighed. "We've been keeping ourselves apart from people in some way our whole lives, haven't we, Savannah? I wonder how hard it's going to be to change that now."

For a moment a bittersweet silence hung in the air between us. Then grunts from downstairs called Reece away again, and by the time he returned I knew there was one more thing I had to raise with him.

"The yellow stripes and the dark mounds," I said. "The ones the doctor saw in my throat at the hospital. I've been wondering if they might be part of some kind of weapon?"

Reece grinned, but it was humorless. "It feels like it, doesn't it? Like a natural part of our body—"

"But dangerous to the monster." It was hard saying the word *monster* so bluntly like that, but afterwards I was glad. The shared dreams proved that it wasn't just some imaginary fear. "Earlier, I was hoping that maybe we could see for ourselves what's inside our throats," I said hesitantly. "You know, take a proper look without anyone else needing to be involved. Just us. No strangers."

"But now you're not so sure we can get close enough, eh?" He frowned. "You're right, though. We should try. I wonder if I can keep my own lips open long enough to let you see what's in my throat?" He sounded as if he was trying to convince himself. "Maybe. I'll have a go, anyway. What's the best way to do this? I know. Let's not make it complicated. I'll just lie down and let you look inside my mouth."

He dropped flat on his back, the mattress bouncing under his weight.

I smiled as Reece glanced at me expectantly, but how could we do this safely? The obvious thing was just to peer straight into his mouth, but that meant getting close to his face, and after what had happened to Carol I didn't want to risk that. Reece wasn't finding it easy keeping his lips open, either. As I hovered nervously over him, his jaw muscles kept tensing, straining to keep his teeth from coming together. I found myself having to say "wider" in the same way the ENT doctor had earlier.

"I still can't see what's in there," I whispered, my own neck, directly above his, feeling hopelessly exposed. "It's too dark."

He yanked the curtains over the bed wider for more light. "Keep trying," he groaned. "I want to know what it is as much as you."

I lowered myself further, but doing so suddenly made me feel totally defenseless. At the same time my throat begun to simmer menacingly. Sensing it was about to strike out at Reece, I pulled back.

A flood of relief washed across his face. "*Yes, stay where you are,*" he murmured in a strangled tone, as if he really wanted me to. Then he grit his teeth. "Sorry," he muttered. "I'm just—this is difficult. Look, let's do it another way. I can see your mouth well from this angle. The light from the window's shining right on it. How wide can you get your own lips?"

I tried parting them, but at the same moment I suddenly knew my throat was about to attack Reece.

"No," I gasped. Jerking away sharply, I backed into the wall, accidentally knocking off one of his portraits.

"I can't," I whispered. "I'm sorry, Reece. I know it was my idea, but I just can't. I'm . . . I'm leaving. I have to go."

"What? Right now?" Reece stood up, looking confused. "All right. "I'll . . . let you out."

I scrambled past him. I tried to stay calm, but the hostile signals my body was giving me were overwhelming. I knew Reece was in danger if I stayed. I couldn't risk that.

"I scared you, didn't I?" he said, sounding spooked as he followed me down. "That's the last thing I meant to do."

"It's OK," I told him. "Just let me go."

At the bottom of the stairs I felt an arm on mine, holding me back. It belonged to Mr. Gandolfo. I pulled away from him, yanking open the front door.

"Huuuuu," Mr. Gandolfo said—a horrible guttural noise. "Huuuu-eeth." With tiny shuffles of his bandaged feet he attempted to follow me.

Reece winced. "It's all right, Dad. Savannah's going." He stressed this to him patiently and repeatedly.

Mr. Gandolfo didn't listen. He kept frantically mouthing at me.

"He's trying to say good-bye," Reece said. "I know it looks odd, but that's all it is. He's thanking you for coming. It's important to him. We don't get many visitors." He bit his lip. "When will I see you again?"

"Soon." I didn't trust my throat enough to say anything more while we were still close. I just raced out of the house. I didn't even stay long enough to be civil to Mr. Gandolfo. I plunged up their stone path, gulping air.

"I'll ring you!" I called back. "I'm sorry. It's not you, Reece . . . it's me . . . it's me. . . . "

"It's both of us," he said. "It's OK, Savannah. I know how you feel. I do."

I desperately wanted to talk to him, explain my feelings, but my body wouldn't let me. It made me run. And by the time I was halfway up the street and turned around again the door to Reece's house had shut.

Mr. Gandolfo hadn't quite gone, though. His legs were still visible behind the frosted glass panel of the door. His bony knees were tight up against the pane, his thighs pressed like blobs of pale flesh against the glass. Then the blobs retreated, and his black bathrobe swayed just once across the doorway before that vanished too.

9

Precambrian Earth: the longest eon in our world's history. For three billion years, all the Ocrassa had to feed upon were tiny microorganisms: protozoa, bacteria, protists, fungi, archaea.

Even so, while the Ocrassa consumed their tiny bodies, it took the best each had to offer and used them to improve itself.

Grasping the whiplike flagella of a bacterium, it was able to propel itself around, but it remained in the dark until it blundered across the first examples of euglena algae. These had simple, light-sensitive cells, but the algae did little with them except avoid shadows. The Ocrassa covered the cells with a thin transparent layer, and in doing so gave itself a primitive eye.

And suddenly—instantly—the Ocrassa became the best hunter in its domain. Other organisms tried to flee or fight back, but the Ocrassa was always a step ahead of their evolution. They relied on random genetic mutation to improve. The Ocrassa simply took the best from each organism it came across and used it *efficiently.*

Then, still voiceless, but already an insatiable traveler, the Ocrassa left its shallow watery pool and plunged into a deep warm sea. It was a risky strategy, for this was an environment it did not know, but its reward was to find far more advanced animals: jellyfish, corals, and anemones.

The Ocrassa adapted their bodies to its needs: constructed from them external sensory organs, a nervous system, a valved heart. And once it had those things, the Ocrassa's speed of development was frightening. Pumping blood rapidly through its bright new veins, it traveled faster, found prey sooner, and took what they had to offer.

And always—methodically, implacably, learning all the time—it killed.

Soon nothing in the ocean could evade it. The Ocrassa became a vast, hungry, wave-scavenger. But it remained dissatisfied. Driven by its genes, its goal was to reach the apex of the food chain.

To get there, it gave up millions of years of domination of the oceans and, without a moment's regret, switched its attention back to the land.

Above a gravel beach it stumbled across plants. Dimensions are important, and for a while the Ocrassa was mesmerized by the sheer size of a fern. Ferns could draw water and nutrients from the ground. To the

Ocrassa—which had always had to swim or scramble to find its food—they appeared to be a superior form.

The Ocrassa became a fern, but kept its eyes. The eyes dotted the stem, watchful, staring at waving fronds and grey-blue skies.

But this was also the Ocrassa's first serious mistake. For plants are leisurely. They are all slowness and quiet waiting.

And nature, at last, saw its first real chance to fight back. It caused another, larger, fern to choke the light above the Ocrassa. In the past the Ocrassa would simply have flopped or swum to safety, but that was no longer possible. It was a plant, stuck in sluggish movement. Denied sunlight, it delved more roots into the earth, but that took days and there was not enough water.

Nature called forth further plants. They gathered above the Ocrassa. Blocking out the light, they starved it. The Ocrassa began to weaken. More plants assembled. Crowding out the final chinks of sunshine, they stripped what little moisture was left in the soil.

Nature might have killed the Ocrassa then. Nature had only to wait. But it made a crucial mistake. It threw the most advanced life-forms that existed at that time against the Ocrassa. Arthropods, copepods, and mites—tiny insects that fed on plant matter—were sent in to issue the death blows.

In they came: crawling, aggressive, a horde.

The Ocrassa was eaten alive. Its leaves were chewed, its

precious eyes gnawed. But even while the insects gorged, the Ocrassa had found something new to study, and it did so, spellbound by the possibilities they represented. Invading the body of one of the mites, it suddenly seized control. Then, still half-plant in its DNA, the Ocrassa picked up its eight new springy mite legs, scuttled away, and hid.

For a while the Ocrassa rested, getting used to the feel of the mite's unfamiliar body. Then it set about upgrading it. It deepened the minuscule eyes. Reinforced the skin. Strengthened the legs. The mite's mouthparts were already gloriously sharp, even without improvements, but of course the Ocrassa made improvements.

And, as it changed its form—dissecting flesh, sculpting new limbs—for perhaps the first time in its already ancient life the Ocrassa looked backwards instead of forwards. It had a dim sense of an emotion it would later identify as hatred for the plants. They had canopied it with darkness. They had denied it light, denied it moisture. The arthropods, copepods, and mites were long departed, but the plants could not so easily flee.

Taking its time, the Ocrassa adapted its mite-jaws and began to gnaw at the surrounding fern roots. It did so in complex ways that would prolong the plants' agony for as long as possible. The Ocrassa knew exactly how to do so. After all, it had once been one of them.

It became a cannibal.

10

After leaving Reece's house, I paced frantically around the surrounding streets, half out of my mind with fear. Where was I supposed to go now? How could I go any-where with my throat threatening everyone?

I cringed, appalled by the way I'd left Reece. He'd trusted me. Opened his mouth. Exposed his neck. And how had I repaid that trust? By panicking. By running away like a little girl.

I can't handle this, I thought. *I can't. I can't.*

Looking up, I saw that the sky was again full of leaves. There were so many that I had to kick them out of my path. *Leave me alone*, I thought furiously, not wanting to think about their meaning now, fearing what it might be.

A few minutes later a text came from Reece.

"I'm sorry. I don't know what I was thinking of, making you lean over me like that."

"Don't apologize," I texted back. "It was my idea, not yours. I'll phone later."

I chose a backstreet route to Nina's, but it was still hard to avoid people, and by the time I reached her house I'd reached a decision. I couldn't go on like this. I couldn't spend the rest of my life hiding, scared to get close to people. One way or another I had to know what was inside me.

Nina wanted to know all the details of what had happened over at Reece's, but after giving her the basics I rooted through my bag for my mobile phone and activated the camera.

"What's that for?" she asked.

"I need to see it for myself."

She stared at me, incredulous. "You're going to take a *picture* of it?"

"I'm going to try."

"Sav, don't," she begged. "You don't know what's in there. It could be anything. Go back to the hospital. Let Olly check . . ."

But I didn't dare. I couldn't let anyone poke around inside my throat. Not until I knew what was inside. Eventually I persuaded Nina of that, and she reluctantly helped me fiddle with the mobile's camera-flash setting, adjusting it to automatic.

Once she'd done that, I walked into the bathroom. Despite Nina's objections, I went alone, and insisted on locking the door behind me. Nina argued, wanting to stay closer, but there was no way I was taking a chance of hurting her. *Get on with it*, I told myself, filled with dread as I blinked at my reflection in the bathroom's mirror. *Just do it. You've got to see what's in there.*

The first photo proved the hardest to take. My hand was shaking so much the lens wouldn't focus. Keeping my jaw wide made me whimper as well, and I had to keep reassuring Nina on the other side of the bathroom door that I was OK when I wasn't. But I finally managed to take three snapshots. The first two were unfocused and useless. In the third my lips came out as blurry as on the others, but further down my throat I'd luckily managed to capture . . . details.

I immediately saw the honey-colored bands the doctor had mentioned. They were two luminous stripes, each about a centimeter wide, running right down the middle of my throat.

Panting with fear, I examined the photo more closely.

And that's when I glimpsed the *mounds*.

There were two frighteningly large masses of flesh on either side of my throat. Each was a glistening chocolate-brown in color, the contrast with the surrounding ordinary pink of my skin startling. The flesh on them had an oddly taut, stretched look as well, as if it was under great pressure.

I was still reeling from the sight of the mounds when I realized that something else was down there. A large object. Something Dr. Edilman had missed. Something that must have *tucked itself* out of sight when she examined me.

It let me see it now, though—and I shrieked.

"Sav, what are you doing?" Nina pleaded, rattling the door handle.

"Stay out," I gasped. "Nina, whatever you do, don't try to come in."

The photo didn't give me anywhere near enough information to know what I was looking at. For a moment I was glad of that. Then I realized that no matter how scared I was, I had to find a way to see it better. Needing more light to shine down my throat, I used a hand mirror from one of the shelves to angle sunlight directly from the window. I still couldn't quite see what was below the mounds, though, until I had the idea of shaking my head.

That's when I saw the object *billow*.

Delicate flaps of skin wafted slowly up from the inner surface of my throat, and then fell back, equally slowly, on an internal breeze.

Yelping in shock, for a couple of minutes I just fell hard onto the toilet seat in a hot sweat, fending off Nina's desperate attempts to get me out of the bathroom.

Then I prodded my neck in the area I'd seen the object. It felt loose—fragile.

With my heart pounding, I suddenly realized the truth: the billowing thing—combined with the honey-colored stripes and mounds—*was the weapon*. I even sensed how the parts worked together. The flaps of skin created the sounds, the mounds amplified them, and the stripes focused and *launched* them. It was terrifying being so sure of that, but when I thought about it I was even more terrified because now, of course, I couldn't cling on to the possibility that they meant something else. There could be only one reason for having a weapon like this inside me.

There really *was* a monster out there.

Breathing out heavily, I tapped in Reece's number and sent the photo to him. Then I passed the mobile under the crack of the bathroom door and waited for the inevitable reaction from Nina.

She said nothing for a minute. Then, when I unlocked the door, she slid the mobile back across the floor. When she finally stepped inside, my back was to her and I was scared to turn around. Nina came in front of me and when I eventually managed to lift my chin I saw that her face was almost white with fear. She wordlessly handed the mobile back, and for a second I thought she was going to be sick. But somehow she held herself together and stood beside me.

All I wanted to do in that moment was bury my face in her arms, but I didn't dare.

"C'mon, let me see it," she demanded. "I mean it. Open your lips, Sav. I'm gonna . . . gonna have a real look. I've got to. I can't stay with you if I don't know what it looks like. I'll be too frightened. You've got to let me see it."

She leaned towards me, but I snapped *no* so hard that she froze.

"Savannah Grey, you . . . what are you doing? Listen to me," Nina almost shouted. "Just you listen. . . . " She was crying. "You can't go on like this. No way you can. Even if you're careful, someone's going to—I don't know—accidentally brush up against you. They're bound to, aren't they? Touch you by mistake. Something like that. What's going to happen if they do? You'll hurt them. You've got to get rid of it!"

"I can't do that," I told her, my own tears flowing freely.

"For God's sake, Sav—" But before she could say anything else my mobile bleeped.

It was a photo from Reece. A mobile snapshot of his throat.

I stared at it for several seconds, shivers cascading down my back. In the photo Reece was gazing at the camera, his tongue held down with a pencil. It was such a clear picture that I was able to read *HB* stenciled in tiny letters on the side. Beyond the pained expression in his eyes the contents of his throat were chillingly laid out. They were similar to mine. The main difference was size. His honey-colored bands were less than a third the brightness of mine, the glistening chocolate-brown mounds nearly nonexistent. And lower down, around his vocal cords—where his scar tissue was—there was almost nothing at all.

He'd added the following note:

Everything in my throat looks underdeveloped nxt to yrs. I'm way behind u. Dad did more damage than any1 knew. Call when yr ready. Anytime.

I showed Reece's photo to Nina. She shook her head at it for a long time, so scared that her tears dried up. "Sav," she pleaded, desperately trying to find a way to get through to me, "you've got to find out what that thing in there is. You've got to get it cut out!"

"I can't."

"Why not? *Why not?*"

"Because—" But how could I make her understand when I didn't understand myself? "Because . . . I don't know . . . because . . . I think I need it."

"What?" Nina compressed her lips. "Sav, it's *growing* inside you!"

"Please," I said, almost on my knees. "Please, just help me, Nina. Don't shout. I need you on my side."

"I *am* on your side," she groaned. "Of course I am! But listen to what you're saying. You can't leave something like that in your body. It could be killing you—"

"It's not killing me."

"You don't know that! You don't know *anything* about it. You can't even eat properly anymore."

"It's harder to eat," I admitted, "but . . . I still can. I think . . . whatever it is, it's there to protect me, Nina." I was shaking. We'd argued plenty of times before, but never like this. I was frightened I'd lose her unless I could make her understand. "Nina, it's really fragile." That sounded so feeble, but I couldn't think of another way to describe it. "It's . . . I think it's easily injured. When you see it, when you really look at it, you can tell how frail it is. Delicate, somehow."

That didn't get the reaction I expected. Whatever Nina saw in my expression obviously shocked her, because she said, "Oh God, you *like* it being there, don't you?"

"It's not that," I murmured, staring at the floor.

"No, you do. I can tell." A shiver of sheer revulsion crossed her face. "Oh, Sav, you're happy to let it keep growing in there, aren't you? You think it's something *precious*."

||

I took Nina's chilling question to bed with me that night.

Was she right? Did I like what was in my throat? No. Of course not. I didn't want some kind of object growing inside me. But it wasn't a simple matter of liking or disliking, was it? No matter how scared I was, I couldn't just scream and wish this all away. More than ever now, I was convinced there was a monster out there, and if that was true what else did Reece and I have to defend ourselves other than whatever was inside our throats?

I rang him, and after the fraught argument with Nina, his calmer voice came as such a relief. We spoke for hours, comparing the photos in more detail, and though Reece sounded just as scared by the images as I, he shared my view about not going back to King's. "But maybe we should try experimenting a bit more?" he suggested. "You know, coughing, seeing what noises we can make with our throats, that kind of thing. If it's a weapon, maybe we can get control of it."

We tried, but all that came from my lips were thin rasps, and it was the same for Reece.

It was very late when I finally ended the call, and I almost rang him straight back again. The last thing I wanted to do was spend the rest of the night on my own. *So call Nina*, I thought. *Call her.* But like all the other times I'd started to do so tonight, I stopped halfway through keying in her number. More than anything I wanted to talk to her, patch things up between us, but it felt too soon after the bitter way we'd argued earlier. Anyway, knowing Nina, she'd probably already made plans to turn up first thing in the morning with reinforcements to drag me back to the hospital.

I finally turned my light off around three a.m., but I was way too edgy to sleep. And perhaps that was fortunate because soon afterwards a sound floated up from downstairs.

Scamper and stop.

And accompanying the scamper was a splash. A squirt of liquid—as if something was dribbling wetly onto the hard surface of the stairs.

I sat bolt upright, listening intently. For a while there were no more sounds, except a murmur that sounded a bit like *pas pas*, but was so faint it might have been anything. Blinking in the darkness, I was tempted to wake Annette, but I didn't. Instead I clung pathetically to the hope that an ordinary animal like a rodent was in the house.

Scamper and stop.

There it was again—followed this time by a sigh. I was sure it was a sigh. Could animals sigh? I got the impression something large was below me, poised at the foot of the stairs.

"I hear you," I murmured—and inside my throat something eased open in readiness.

The silence that followed was terrifying. Doubly terrifying, because surely an animal would have moved again. It wouldn't have showed such patience.

In the end I knew the only one way to be certain nothing was in the house was to check. Sliding from the sheets, I buttoned up my nightshirt and walked barefoot to the bedroom door.

The corridor was empty.

So was the staircase.

Annette's door was shut. Soft, familiar snores came from inside.

Switching on all the corridor lights, I paced warily to the end of the hall. Then I made my way downstairs, searching all the rooms on the ground floor.

Nothing.

I returned to my own room, but didn't go back to bed. Instead I sat on top of my duvet, the door ajar, listening.

It was around an hour later that the scampering started up again. Quick, light steps they were, darting about, and this time they came from the upper part of the house. I heard a footfall, then a leap between stairs, followed by a body landing with a distinct *crump* near my room.

"Who's there?" I whispered.

"Pas pas!" came a high-pitched, breathy answer. "Pas de bourrée!"

Stifling a scream, I jumped out of bed. For a second I hesitated. Then I yanked the door wide.

There was a scuttle, a quick flash of bobbing blonde hair. Then, as I ran down the corridor, something odd happened to my eyes. They began fast-flickering. At first I thought it was just nervousness—that I was shaking—but it wasn't that. Both my eyes were rapidly changing their focus. They were doing so from second to second, an efficient sweep of the space ahead of me. It was similar to the feeling I'd experienced yesterday when looking out at the leaves, but if anything the sensation now was even more vivid. *I'm seeing better,* I realized. And perhaps that should have frightened me, except in that moment I knew I needed it. *To catch a monster, you have to be able to see it. This one doesn't want to be seen.*

As if to confirm this, my eyes were restless—after something. I let them lead me gradually along the corridor.

It wasn't until I reached the top of the staircase that I saw the handprint on the landing window. It was a fresh handprint, thick and yellowish, about the size of a child's. Checking more closely, though, I saw that the outline wasn't like a child's at all. The hand was too wide, the thumb and index finger excessively elongated. And the last three fingers were fused together.

Glancing over my shoulder—afraid that whatever it was had slinked behind me—I placed my own fingers on top of the outline to better gauge its size.

And a shudder passed down my spine.

The handprint was *sticky*. Not a standard perspiring kind of stickiness. It felt tactile, warm, almost alive. There was an odor to the liquid as well. A faint oiliness. Nothing human—or any animal I knew—smelled remotely like this.

Furiously wiping my hand on my nightshirt, I craned my neck down the staircase. Whatever creature was in the house, I sensed it was extraordinarily dangerous. My roving eyes supported that conclusion. They were agitated, darting about, sensitive to the tiniest air motions.

Checking on Annette—opening her bedroom door—I was relieved to find her still sleeping soundly. Good. At least she was safe.

It was only as I was backing out of the shadows of her room that a body lunged behind me.

My hands instantly rose to shield my neck. At the same time I spun around. The hallway was empty, but my eyes detected movement. The wire from the ceiling's central light fixture was swaying. Something had just traveled past it. There was also a small yellow drip on the staircase. It hadn't been there a moment ago. As I stepped towards it, I felt rather than saw something big scuttling away incredibly fast.

Leaping down the stairs, I was just in time to see a dog-like creature disappearing out the front door.

A doglike creature with a star-shaped head.

For a moment I was too shocked to do anything.

Then a sound erupted from my throat.

It was a low-pitched *slither*. Thrusting from my mouth at remarkable speed, it welled out towards the darkness of the open doorway. The sound wasn't loud, but it was so penetrating that the star-headed creature, fleeing around a corner, screamed as the sound caught up with it.

By the time I made it to the front door, however, the creature was gone.

I was too scared to go after it. Instead I stayed in the garden for hours, watching and listening. It was around dawn that my throat, quietly, mysteriously, began to whir. It was such an eerie sound, a *thrum* running like a cool pulse up and down my neck. But as intensely frightened by it as I was, part of me welcomed it as well, because what else did I have to threaten the creature with? And when a particularly loud set of *clicks* suddenly sprang to my lips, I wondered if it might even be a warning, and staggered across the dewy grass to look over the garden fence. I half-expected to spot the star-headed creature on its way back, but all I could see were leaves. Leaves everywhere. The entire block was heaving with them. Willow. Yew. Larch. Cedar. Hazel. So many different species. Most weren't even from this area. How far had they traveled to get here?

Returning to my bedroom, I propped my face in my hands and gazed out over the garden. There had to be a reason why so many trees were shedding everywhere. Until now I'd assumed the leaves were something to do with the monster from my dreams, but were they? Maybe it was an attempt to communicate.

Was I being sent a message?

I studied the leaves, searching for a meaning. The amber streetlights were dull, but with my sharper eyes I could still pick out all the leaves' delicate veins. I saw them tremble, the way they shivered in the wind. Gusts carried them back and forth, and even as I watched, another heavy swirl, silver birch this time, scudded over the house. So many hurrying, frantic-looking leaves. Lime and elm. Ash and chestnut. Holly.

For a moment I thought of the star-headed creature, and wondered if it, too, was somewhere out there in the darkness, quietly gathering itself. And then, relaxing my sight, I gazed up again at the night sky. A tangled line of ivy was passing over my chimney. Their jagged leaves dwindled slowly over the neighborhood, tossed on the wind. In the far distance they were joined against the backdrop of stars by another leaf-stream, and another, and another.

Some of the leaves paused to circle my house before they flew on. Most, though, sailed directly eastwards, towards some unknown destination. It was an incredible sight, like a migration: a vast journey of fervent greens, bitter browns, and luminous oranges, all rustling across one another as they fluttered towards the rising dawn. And I had an urge to be amongst them. I had a strong urge to go outside. To follow the leaves, see where they led. But I didn't. I was too scared.

Because what was the star-headed creature if not a monster?

12

Four meters long, pincered, and festooned with teeth: by the Cambrian Era the Ocrassa had become a voracious killer.

Sleek and gilled for underwater hunting, it was equally adept on land. Light slithered off its skin. In darkness, nothing could see it. On its back legs alone it carried sixteen eyes. They were wasteful of energy, but they ensured no creature ever caught it by surprise. By day it hunted, and by night. It fed all the time. Weather was irrelevant. In cold times it sprouted fur and wrapped a tongue around its face to keep warm. During hot nights it could sweat even from its lips.

Nature, however, constantly opposed it. Actively seeking to kill the Ocrassa, it made use of the latest, most advanced animals. Each attack failed, but from the attacks the Ocrassa learned that nature, too, could adapt.

Over time, new species proliferated across the earth. The Ocrassa plucked one from the air—a primitive damselfly.

On its back was something superb: thin, astonishingly light membranes, separated by blood-filled veins.

The first wings.

Their span was over a meter.

More excited by this than anything it had come across before, the Ocrassa shaped its own body to fit the wings. And then, glorying in the sky, it soared.

Eventually there was nothing it could not track or eat on the face of the earth. When the age of the great dinosaurs arrived, the Ocrassa gifted itself the speed of a theropod and the bite-force of a megalosaurus. It made itself into one of the heaviest creatures ever to live on the planet, but it was not slow. Indeed, killing became so easy that for a while the Ocrassa ate only when it could trick things into its jaws. Dinosaur babies scurried into its safe-smelling mouth, thinking it was Mother.

This was predatory perfection of a kind, but the Ocrassa remained dissatisfied. Seeking forever to improve itself, it changed again, radically this time: gave itself vocal cords, taught itself language. The result was extraordinary. By merely developing a vocabulary—learning to name objects and events, to categorize—the Ocrassa increased its brain capacity tenfold. It loved the result, using its enhanced mind to learn. And because there is no faster or better way, it learned like a child—passionately, wholeheartedly, trying everything.

But it also took a backward step for a time because inevitably the growing brain of the Ocrassa also gave it...an imagination.

And with that the Ocrassa experienced its first loneliness. On dark nights, comprehending how unique and ancient it was, it began to dwell on the possibility of its own death. And because the old always fear the end more than the young, its life was punctuated by moments of terror it had never known before.

Desperate to feel safe again, it spent an age in experiments matching its great bulk to flight symmetries. The result was vast dry wings it could escape on, despite its huge mass, if it had to.

It never had to.

Instead, it became sleeker and faster.

The newly emerging species of birds at the end of the dinosaur age offered better optics than anything it had come across before. The size of a gazelle, but with eighty limbs (it had increased their number and flexibility) the Ocrassa took off excitedly, springing high into the sky, delighting in its new, binocular, forward-vision.

And it killed. Always it killed. Over time it looked only to do so more consummately, in more remarkable ways, with flair. It never showed mercy. Encoded within its DNA was enjoyment of all death apart from its own.

And the day finally arrived when the Ocrassa gained its first true understanding that it was hated by all living things on the planet. That it was friendless, detested, despised. In another intelligent species this might have been a devastating blow. For the Ocrassa it was a moment of revelation. Pleasure hormones—endorphins and serotonins—most of which had been deliberately held back for this moment, were released in a torrent, sending a jolt of pure joy shuddering through every cell of the Ocrassa's body.

This was the first joy it had ever felt. From this moment onward, the Ocrassa would always associate being alone with being content. Solitude meant harmony. Isolation was bliss. No other intelligent creature in the universe had ever developed this evolutionary capability to such a spectacular extent.

It was what made the Ocrassa so terrifying—its ability to forever act alone, to need or want nothing but itself.

For an invading alien species, it was the ultimate evolutionary step.

The Ocrassa had come of age.

13

Throughout the early morning, I kept returning to my bedroom window, haunted by the mystery of the leaves and by the meaning of the star-headed creature. What was it? And what did it want?

Around breakfast time, Nina phoned Annette in an attempt to force me to go to the hospital. I was in the middle of trying to resist Annette without going into what I'd seen last night, when my mobile rang.

"There's something outside," said the voice at the other end. Reece, and his voice was a whisper. "It's sort of like a dog, but it's not a dog, no way it's a dog."

I felt my stomach clench. "Where is it?"

"In one of the garden trees. It's just looking at me. It's got spikes instead of a head."

"Stay where you are," I told him, grabbing my shoes and hastily explaining what I'd seen last night. "Don't go out. Don't do anything until I get there."

I hurried, but by the time I reached Reece's house the star-headed creature was gone. Part of me felt relief that I didn't have to face it, but at the same time all I could think was: *it knows where we both live.* All night I'd been worried about how much danger I was in personally, but this second sighting made me realize that everyone I knew was at risk. Annette would be defenseless against anything that moved so fast. Nina, too. And though we'd touched lightly around the subject last night on the phone, how safe was Reece? His throat-weapon wasn't anywhere near as developed as mine. His dad's knife had damaged him badly. *I have to find a way to protect him as well*, I thought. But how could I even begin to do that without knowing what the star-headed creature wanted?

Still looking stunned, Reece pointed from his bedroom window. "It was just sitting out there," he said. "It was sort of flapping these tiny little arms in the middle of its chest, and humming to itself. Then, when it saw me, it waved."

"*Waved?*" That sent a cold sensation through me.

The star-headed creature had left yellow drips everywhere. They were all over Reece's windowsill and the outer brickwork. Without handholds, it had also apparently climbed down the sheer wall below his bedroom. What kind of creature could do that?

The yellow drips were easy enough to follow into the garden, but ended abruptly at the gate. *It concealed its trail.* Goose bumps ran up my arms. *It's intelligent enough to do that.*

Reece was dressed in a black and gold track suit. "I was about to go on a training run at Battersea," he muttered, looking pale. "Maybe I should still go. Yeah, let's get out of the house, Savannah. If that creature's after us, I don't want Dad accidentally coming across it. The way he is right now, just seeing it might be enough to kill him."

I agreed. I doubted Mr. Gandolfo was a target, but I couldn't be sure. In any case, hadn't the star-headed creature already proven how expert it was at hiding inside a house? It could be here right now and I might never see it. The big open spaces of Battersea Park felt safer. If the star-headed creature approached us there it would be easier to spot. And maybe, just maybe, there'd be a chance to follow it as well and see where it went.

By the time we arrived at Battersea Park's sports ground, half a dozen other boys were already doing warm-ups and leg stretches on the athletics track. "That's James McCarthy, my coach," Reece said, indicating a paunchy middle-aged man with an ugly, heavily wrinkled face across the field. "I'll just let him know I'm here."

I nodded and stationed myself warily on a nearby bench while Reece took his place alongside the other boys. He started his training session, and I didn't interrupt. I just kept him in sight while he limbered up.

Come on, I thought, my eyes flicking among the park trees. *Show yourself.*

While I phoned Annette and Nina to check they were OK, Reece jogged eight circuits of the track. By the time he finished he was only slightly winded. I watched him with folded arms. *You really are an athlete, aren't you?* I realized, seeing the grace with which he ran. You're much better than the rest of the boys. That's why McCarthy's interested in you. You're the youngest here, but you're still the best athlete. Was that a coincidence? Somehow I doubted it, and it gave me an idea.

I pointed to a monitor on Reece's wrist. "What's that used for?"

"It measures your heartrate," he told me, his eyes fixed anxiously on the nearest trees. "Everything in fitness is compared against a resting pulse. Why do you ask?"

I shrugged, but my mind was racing. Sharper eyes, I thought. Did the rest of my body have something to offer as well?

"What's *your* heart rate?" I asked.

"Normally around sixty-two."

"Is that good?"

"Pretty good, yeah."

"What's mine?" When he showed surprise, I offered him my wrist. "Go on," I said, "check it."

"Is it safe to get that close to you?"

Good question. But my throat wasn't making any threatening noises. "Just do it slowly," I said.

Reece took hold of my wrist *exceptionally* slowly. Then, attaching the monitor, he measured my pulse for ten seconds.

Afterwards, he stayed very still.

"What's wrong?" I asked.

"Nothing. A crazy reading, that's all." A few moments later, after repositioning the device, he said, "This monitor's duff," discarded it, and tested me using his fingers.

He left them on my wrist for about a minute. Despite the close contact, I noticed that there were no warning clicks coming from my throat. It hit me: *He's nowhere near my mouth. That's the difference.* It was such a relief to know we could at least touch like this that as the seconds stretched out I found my tension being replaced by different feelings. More ambivalent ones.

I glanced up. Reece's forehead was perspiring, perhaps from running. So was his hand. Or was it *my* hand?

"This pulse is ridiculous," he said, whipping out his stopwatch. "I'm going to take the reading again. Just breathe naturally."

"I am breathing naturally. What's wrong?"

"I'm not sure yet."

Exactly thirty seconds later Reece dropped my hand in my lap and stepped away, a look of disbelief on his face.

"Your resting heart rate is twenty-eight," he whispered.

"Is that low?"

"Low? It's almost impossibly low. Even the most incredible athletes in the world don't have that kind of resting beat."

I shivered, feeling scared, but also wondering where this might be leading.

"Why don't I join you on a lap or two?" I suggested.

"Around the track?"

"Why not?"

I led the way, and we jogged together three times around the circuit, watched by an irritated coach McCarthy. When we were finished, Reece retested my pulse. This time he hesitated before murmuring, "It's nearly back to forty already. It can't be." Biting his lower lip, he gazed at me with real concern. "Aren't you tired? No, don't answer that. I can see you're not. Jesus, what's going on here?"

He was right. I didn't even feel winded. "What about trying something tougher?" I said. Thinking of the star-headed creature, I knew it was time to push myself. "What's the hardest exercise on your schedule?"

"A twelve-minute run test."

"Let's do it."

Reece led me towards the outside lane of the racetrack. Picking a pedometer off the side of the tarmac, he strapped it around his waist. Then, changing his mind, he strapped it around my waist instead.

"Whooah, tickles," I said, as his hands circled my hips to do the buckle up. He grinned, then concentrated on setting the mode.

"This measures your speed and distance," he said.

While he tightened the belt and set the timer, I looked around the field. There was no sign of the star-headed creature. McCarthy stood on the other side of the track, showing a group of boys an abdominal exercise.

"All we're going to do is run as fast as we can for exactly twelve minutes," Reece explained, stepping back to size me up. "If you get tired slow down, but the point is to try not to stop. OK?" I nodded. "We'll follow the track circuit," he said. "Oh, and if you outpace me in front of the other guys I'll never forgive you." He smiled, showing he didn't mean it. "Ready?"

"Ready."

We started off, and for the first minute or so I maintained the same long-striding tempo as Reece. It was almost a full-on sprint, but not quite.

"You OK?" he asked, looking surprised to see me keeping up.

"I'm fine."

I was better than fine. I wasn't even breathing heavily. My rhythm was smooth and easy. Alongside me, though, Reece began to falter every fourth or fifth stride, and as we got near the ten minute mark he was visibly slowing. I reduced my own pace to stay with him.

"No, push harder!" he gasped. "Forget about pacing yourself. You're finding this easy, aren't you?"

It was true. I wasn't even perspiring. Knowing I had more to give, but not how much, I launched myself harder along the tight bends of the track. Across the field McCarthy's boys, hands on hips, were all clustered around his stopwatch, avidly watching. I had no idea how fast I was going, but abruptly Reece was ahead of me. Without noticing it, I'd almost lapped him.

"Keep going!" he yelled, waving me on. "Forget about limiting yourself to twelve minutes. Just run, Sav!" He looked exhilarated. "How fast can you go?"

With his elation spurring me on, I pushed ahead, eating up section after section of track.

It must have been several minutes later that I started feeling winded, and shortly after that I wanted to stop, so I did. As I strolled across to Reece and McCarthy on the other side of the track all the boys gazed at me in astonishment, forming a path as if I was a celebrity. Reece looked just as awed as the others. I noticed he was still panting heavily, while I was already breathing easily again.

McCarthy elbowed past two boys. "Take her pulse now," be barked.

Reece did so. "Forty-four," he reported triumphantly.

"That's rubbish," McCarthy snapped. "It can't be that low. Let me take it." He held my wrist. After a few seconds he swore. Still holding my wrist, he blinked at the pedometer readout.

"18,578 meters," McCarthy murmured, shaking his head as if he couldn't believe what he was seeing. "She ran 18,578 meters." He stared at me openmouthed, checked the pedometer again. "Even at twelve minutes you'd done

8,547 meters." Seemingly unsure what to say next, he slowly gathered himself. "How regularly do you train?" There was more than a hint of fear in his voice.

"I never exercise," I told him honestly.

"Never?" He tried to take that in. "Are you using performance-enhancing drugs?"

"I don't use any drugs."

"You sure?" He gave me a chance to change my mind. "No steroids?"

"No steroids."

As if McCarthy knew that no amount of performance-improving substances could explain what he'd just seen, he nodded. Then he said in a hushed voice, "I'm not quite sure what I'm meant to tell you at this moment, so I'll just stick to the facts. You've at least doubled what anyone should be able to do. What you achieved on that run is totally unprecedented. In fact, it shouldn't really be possible."

Reece stood next to me, squeezing my hand encouragingly. "How about a *real* sprint?" he said.

"What do you think she's been doing for the last five minutes?" McCarthy growled.

"That wasn't flat-out," Reece replied shrewdly, turning towards me with a look of pride. "I think she's got a lot more in the tank."

He was right. For the first half of the twelve-minute run I'd been taking it easy. I stood beside him, a jumble of emotions. Fear, of course, was the main one. Ever since

I'd seen the star-headed creature, panic had been pouring nonstop through my mind. But when I stared at Reece another emotion wrestled with that. A determination to see where this led. A growing sense of resolve. I clung on to that feeling. I was sick of being scared all the time. If I was about to face a monster, I had to know what else I could do. McCarthy indicated a 35-meter area marked out on the running track used for sprinting. "I'll do it with you," Reece said, positioning himself alongside.

McCarthy cocked his stopwatch.

"*Go!*" he yelled.

There was a fraction of a second of lag as I felt my thighs gearing up. Then I burst along the track. Within three strides I'd passed Reece. A moment later he was no longer in my peripheral vision. There were gasps as I eased to a stop beyond the marker, Reece trailing in my wake.

"Three-point-six seconds," McCarthy squeaked, his eyes fixed in disbelief on his stopwatch. "3.6 bloody seconds!" He was almost crying, he was so happy. "No one's ever run that time before. Do it again! Do it again!"

I did. This time it took 3.4 seconds. The next: 3.5.

McCarthy rubbed his cheek. He looked as if all the air was being squeezed out of him. I repeated the twelve-minute run test—holding nothing back this time—and ran it much faster than before. So fast, in fact, that by the time I jogged back to McCarthy's boys the atmosphere had changed. All that celebrity awe was gone. They just looked frightened now. Only Reece stepped up to me this time as I came off the track.

"It doesn't matter what they think," he whispered in my ear. "You're amazing."

I clung to his words, giving him a weak smile.

With Reece's encouragement, I asked McCarthy to put me through every other test he could. At one point I lay flat on the ground and swiftly bench-pressed 725 kilograms—a feat which scared the life out of the boys. On every other test I graded out unbelievably high, but something else emerged as well: my *swiftness of response* proved to be even more remarkable than my pure speed or power.

Equally, though, I sensed that there *were* limits to what I could do. I just didn't understand what those limits were yet. And knowing that a monster was out there, about to test them in a very different way, made me deeply uneasy.

At Reece's suggestion, I investigated my hand and wrist strength using a machine called a dynamometer. When I gripped it, the result went beyond the maximum the machine was calibrated for. There was total silence from McCarthy at this. Even Reece's previous excitement was replaced by a haunted look. Frowning, he took the dynamometer off me and tested himself. The result was above average for his age, but not remarkably so.

McCarthy called a halt to the tests, and while everyone else took stock, I sat beside a dazed-looking Reece at the side of the track, wondering what he was thinking. "You told me you can see better as well," he said, rousing himself. "Show me what you mean."

I indicated a distant block of flats. "See the top left window? There's a magazine propped up on someone's desk." Reece squinted, double-checking which window I meant. "It's *Newsweek*," I told him. "The headline says: 'Palm Oil Destroying Amazon.'"

"I can't even see the magazine," Reece murmured. "But hold on. Didn't the star-headed creature come to your house at night?"

I nodded.

"So maybe it's nocturnal," he suggested. "How well you can see in the dark?"

It hadn't occurred to me to check that. To do so we used McCarthy's office. His room was enclosed, no windows. Shutting the door, I turned the lights off, and for a split second I wasn't able to see a thing. Then I could. A crack of light at the bottom of the door was enough for me to pick out the planes and hollows of Reece's face. He stood there, blinking vacantly in the gloom.

"Wait," he said. Fumbling around, he found a sweatshirt and covered up the crack until the room was utterly black. "Can you still see?"

"No," I admitted. *So I need some light*, I realized—and finding a weakness like that frightened me. I sensed it was important.

We returned to the sports field, and I could tell Reece was avoiding my gaze. "Let's face it, Sav, I couldn't see at all in that office, not a damn thing," he said. Grimacing, he shook his head. "I haven't got your gifts. All I've got"—he thumbed dejectedly at his throat—"is whatever's left in here. And that's not much, is it?" *I'm not going to be able to help you against the monster*, his expression said, and I silently held his hand, more determined than ever to protect him.

McCarthy joined us again. "This is the final test we're doing today," he said, in the stunned way I was getting used to. Holding a curved plastic tube towards me, he wiped his brow. "We call this the peak flow test. It measures your lung capacity. All you do is take a big breath, place your lips tightly around the outside of the tube and blow."

For the first time since we'd begun, I felt a tremor of unease.

"No," I said. "I'm not putting anything in my mouth."

McCarthy gave me that same quizzical look I'd first seen from Dr. Edilman at the hospital. "There's nothing to it," he reassured me.

"You just breathe out hard, using a huff rather than a full breath."

I glanced at the instrument suspiciously.

Then, as McCarthy pushed it towards my lips, several *tics* ignited in my throat—and suddenly I knew everyone around me was in danger.

I stepped back.

"It's all right, Sav," Reece said quietly.

"Stay where you are," I warned them all.

My body felt primed to strike, and I took another quick step back to make sure I didn't harm anyone. At the same time my eyes began fast-flickering, looking for threats.

My thought-processes were also speeding up. It was an incredible sensation. Within seconds my brain had combined with my eyes to map the geography of the entire park, forming a startlingly detailed picture of all the blind spots and concealed areas. The smallest sounds around us also separated themselves out. I could hear the grinding jaw of Coach McCarthy, the held breaths of the boys. Reece stepped towards me and for a moment he was not Reece at all, but an evaluation: an object moving into my orbit—a risk. Then it was just Reece again, his hand touching mine, reassuring me.

"Let's get out of here," he whispered.

14

The sun was setting as Reece led me to a quieter section of Battersea Park. Finding an empty bench, the two of us slumped together on it, just trying to recover and somehow make sense of everything that had happened. I couldn't stop shaking. The final dregs of exhilaration I'd felt on the racetrack were gone, leaving me with only their implications. Those implications were beginning to filter through my mind like a drug.

Lightning-fast reactions to everything.

Improved hearing.

Improved vision.

Night vision.

All this speed and power.

Even a week ago my body and mind hadn't been anything like this. It could mean only one thing: I was being prepared. Readied to fight. *The monster's nearly here. It's time.*

But I wasn't prepared. I wasn't ready. How could I ever be ready to confront a monster?

Lowering my head, barely able to look at him, I said to Reece, "I saw the way the boys were staring at me. By the end of the testing, they all thought *I* was some kind of monster, didn't they?"

"It doesn't matter what they think," he reassured me, reaching for my hand. "You're the same person you were."

"No, that's not true, Reece." I didn't want any lies now. "I'm not the same person."

"You are. Your body's changing, but you're still the girl I ran after in the rain." And as he said that, he gave me a steady gaze, one that somehow managed to convey, *No matter what happens, I'll never leave you on your own to face this thing.*

Nothing in my life matched the strength Reece gave me in that moment, and I stared into his eyes, a shudder of relief passing through me.

Not sure what else to do, we started walking slowly together around the park's perimeter. At the western end there was a small playground, and I found myself enviously watching a group of little kids chasing each other around the swings. Reece grabbed the merry-go-round for us, but when a mother gave him a disapproving glare, he settled for an empty bench and we sat on it, close but not touching.

From there we stared out across at the expensive houses overlooking the north side of the park. It was getting late, the sun's rays slanting low at the horizon, and a bar of sunlight suddenly burst through a cloud, magically outlining Reece's hair. One curl stuck up, and I had a wild impulse to smooth it down.

We took a wandering route back to the estate. Reece stopped at a kiosk serving coffee, but even between us we hadn't brought enough money for a single cup, so we ended up just watching the local pigeons going around in circles pecking at crumbs.

I darted glances at Reece whenever he wasn't looking.

As we traipsed towards Vauxhall Bridge, he told me more about his life. We'd already touched on some of it over the phone, but this time he mentioned more private things. His memories of his mum. The lively, athletic man his dad had been before the strokes. There were funny stories as well. As a kid Reece had enjoyed frightening people with his scar.

And the longer he talked, the more I noticed a high-pitched squeak entering his voice. "Told you it sometimes goes wonky," he mumbled apologetically. He was embarrassed, but I wasn't. Did he really think that mattered to me? I found myself focusing less on his voice and more on his lips. Studying them. Watching the way he shaped his words. He couldn't quite get them all out. He tussled against wrong-sounding syllables, his cheek muscles clenching. I'd glimpsed the same struggle in him a few times earlier today as well, his words cutting off into splutters, and seeing it again now, I wanted to hold him, tell him it was OK. But I didn't want to embarrass him, so I kept silent, and after a few moments he was himself again, swallowing and smiling with heart-touching awkwardness.

Lifting his face, he said shyly, "I still hardly know this area. The streets are a maze. How do you find your way around?"

"It's not hard," I said. I pointed out reference points he could use as a guide. The larger buildings. My favorite cafés. Little side streets I relied on for short cuts. My old school was in this area, and on impulse I took him to see it. At some point over the last few years it had been converted into a driving instructor test center, but Reece still seemed interested. I showed him a squat brick building with a flat roof. "My classroom," I announced.

"Where did you sit?" he wanted to know, then laughed. "No, don't tell me. Let me guess. At the front. Teacher's pet."

I laughed with him, nodding, and we wandered into another part of the city. I kept yakking away, a steady stream of one-way chatter. I was aware that my words were running on, that I sounded ridiculous, like some droning tourist guide, but I couldn't seem to stop myself. An odd feeling was gripping me. And when I finally ran out of sensible things to say, I bridged the silence by naming the local streets—literally stating their names as we passed. "That one over there's Boyson Road. That's King's Row just behind it. And over there's the Sea

Breeze Fish Bar, you'll like that, they do good fishcakes, and . . ."

And I looked up at Reece's face.

What is it that makes us human? I suddenly wondered. Isn't it love? Isn't it our capacity for love? But how could anyone ever love me like this—my body preparing to meet a monster? And even if they could, how was I meant to love them back if I could only hold my face away like I was doing now from Reece, never letting him close?

I desperately wanted to kiss him in that moment. Knowing that was impossible, though, I settled for finding his fingers. Interlinking them. Feeling his strong hand inside mine. But that wasn't enough, and Reece must have felt the charged atmosphere between us as well, because he came to a stop on the pavement. Stopped and said something to me. I didn't quite catch it. Something about us being physically close. "It doesn't matter if we can't get any nearer than this," he was murmuring. "I don't care, as long as you're OK." He turned to me. "You're wonderful," he said. "You know that, don't you? You're incredible."

I breathed deeply, looking away, not knowing where to look. On the ground leaves drifted around our feet, and to give my head time to stop spinning, I let my shoes play with them. Reece quietly stirred the same leaves, drawing back when a gust briefly divided our faces.

Then he looked at me again. It was just a look. But as he did so I turned towards him as well. The setting sun was at Reece's back, leaving his face in shadow, and out of that shadow I imagined that he bent towards me. I imagined he had no control over his emotions, that they burst like a supernova out of him, his lips like escaped stars rushing towards mine, and that he kissed me, unable to stop himself, and that our throats allowed it, allowed our faces to meet.

But that didn't happen. How could it? We remained apart, our lips not even close. I didn't dare look at Reece in that moment, and seconds later a cool breeze shot over our cheeks as the last of the sun fell below the horizon.

15

In Dulwich Wood, less than five kilometers from Reece and Savannah, leaves smothered a clearing. For days they had been gathering here, in greater and greater numbers. Every now and again a camouflaged shape—a monster—emerged from or returned to a hole in the woodland soil. Whenever it did so the leaves assaulted it. Their serrated edges aimed for the monster's eyes, but with grotesque swiftness it always eluded them. And this time, as it returned once again unharmed to its lair, the leaves fell still.

Alder and wild cherry were here. Poplar and juniper. Rowan, bay willow, and hornbeam. Every tree had given up something. The leaves flapped like homeless birds among the boughs. They were a whispering discourse. A companionship. A pattern of leaf and wind the like of which the world had never seen before.

And now, in a single motion, a new breeze swept them skyward. For a moment the leaves hovered gloriously, waiting for the right gusts to fling them forth.

And then with a fervid grace they rose together, and headed for Savannah Grey.

16

Reece wanted to check on his dad, so I met with Nina in town. She chose Alfredo's, the quietest café in the shopping area.

The sky was darkening by the time we arrived. Apart from a few chatting kids the only customers were a table of harassed-looking mums and their young kids. Nina ordered the same toasted cheese and ham sandwich she always had at Alfredo's, as if nothing was wrong with the world, but I saw that she was trembling. There had been a sadness between us ever since our argument. Somehow, though, with the din of ordinary shoppers on the street outside, everything seeming so normal, that sadness and all the fear sort of ambushed us both.

But she'd still come. She could have made up an excuse, found a reason to stay away from me, but she hadn't. Even when I told her about the star-headed creature—and I could see how much that scared her—she fumbled for my hand and held it. "Reece," she whispered. "I can see how much he means to you. Let's get out of here. Let's go and see him together."

It was as she was dropping enough money on the table to cover the bill that the shadow began to drift over the café. A little green-eyed boy sitting on the knee of one of the mothers spotted it first. "An eclipse?" someone wondered, the shadow was so colossal, but it wasn't an eclipse. My first thought was *monster*, and at once my throat flared up to guard me.

The shadow was a huge oval haze. Spreading from the south, its ill-defined edges shimmered like a cloud-margin caught in sunshine, and for one heart-relieving second I thought we were safe after all, that it really was just an unusual cloud formation.

Then I heard the noise coming from its heart.

A murmur of leaves.

A percussion of soft rustling.

The oval haze stopped when it was directly over the café. For a moment, the leaves circled and moiled inside, as if making sure we were there. Then fragments started tearing away from the base, shooting downward in a dagger-fast line.

"They're heading . . . towards us," Nina said in a voice that was still more puzzled than frightened.

No, I thought, *they're heading for me.*

The café door was partially ajar. Nina slammed it shut and yanked me further inside. But I couldn't stay there. Accompanied by shouts of fear from everyone, I eluded Nina's grasp and reopened the door.

"What are you doing?" she shrieked.

I didn't know. I only knew I had to be outside, amongst the leaves. Separating myself from the others, I waited alone at the brink of the doorway, facing outward.

And the leaves came for me. They swung down not in some dreamy flutter, but on a hard, accurate wind that seared the streets. So many leaves were there that within seconds the pavements were deluged, and moments later all traffic had to stop. And while drivers screeched to a halt, winding up their windows—adults everywhere shouting in fear—children were doing the opposite, running around in excitement, trying to catch the leaves. The little green-eyed boy scurried past me, scooping up gleeful fistfuls.

But it was my attention the leaves were after. A volley of sycamore suddenly stung my face, and the next moment my head was being turned by their leaf-edges, my face twisted eastwards, my eyes held open.

I was about to follow where they led, but Nina held me back. Thinking I was under attack, she seized my waist. "No, let me go!" I tried to tell her, but over the wind and rustling she couldn't hear me, and even if she could have I think she'd have held on. With a strength born of sheer loyalty to me she fought the leaves to haul me back into the café, banging the door shut.

It was only then, hand rising up, that her finger accidentally caught my chin.

Struck it. Pierced the gap between my upper and lower lip.

Went inside.

Boom. My neck shuddered.

No, I thought, with a terrible sense of foreboding.

Knowing Nina was in danger, but not what that danger was yet, I backed off. But before I could distance myself from her another explosion inside my neck hurled me across the floor, and what happened next made everyone's eyes widen in panic. There were no warm chimes or experimental musical scales this time. Instead, the nerves of my front teeth were flayed as a rapid set of *crackles* sprayed into the café.

Everyone inside paused whatever they were doing and stared at me. The green-eyed boy, not understanding the danger, clapped his hands in delight, as if I'd just performed some kind of wondrous trick. But he stopped clapping when he heard what came next: short, sharp *clack-clacks*, building swiftly in tempo.

I slapped a hand over my lips to prevent the noises emerging, but my other hand removed it. They wanted my mouth *open*.

With no idea what was going to happen next, or how to stop it, I tried to get out of the café, but I couldn't even do that. Detonations inside my neck kept knocking me to the floor.

Then, without warning, four lightning-fast blisters of sound suddenly blazed from my lips. As everyone in the café shrieked, covering their ears, I took my chance, groping for the door, but I never made it. Another concussive boom threw me back, and this time a fever-pitched note drilled out so diamond-hard that the green-eyed boy yelped like a dog, his eyes screwed up in agony.

Nina was still the person closest to me. I desperately motioned for her to keep away, but she didn't understand. She thought I was asking for help. I clenched my lips, but they refused to stay sealed. I knew why. The weapon was ready. Nina had triggered it, and though that had been an accident, whatever was in my throat had found its purpose, and now no force on earth was going to stop my lips opening like the entrance to a cave of horrors.

Collapsing to the ground again, I scrambled across the tiles, using my nails, crawling—anything to get away from Nina—but as my lungs sucked in a great final snatch of preparatory air I knew it was too late. "Not here!" I screamed, barely able to hear my own voice over the din. "Not Nina!"

Unable to stand, I looked around for the exit. The noises from my throat were now unbearably loud. The enclosing walls of the café seemed to be acting like an echo chamber, magnifying the sounds. And already my eyes were on the move: fast-flickering, sweeping the room, seeking a target.

There is no target, I thought furiously. *What are you doing? There's no monster here.*

But I could do nothing as my throat abruptly contracted, and the next thing I knew my neck was being twisted around to face everyone in the room. At the same time my tongue flexed like a directional rod, and all the while my head was still turning, turning with a horribly slow precision. My eyes were the focal point of that precision, selecting and classifying faces in the room: the green-eyed boy, his mother, Nina, a girl clutching her boyfriend.

Then my throat spasmed outward—seeking something specific to strike. *There's nothing here*, I thought despairingly. *There is no target. Not here. Not now. Stop.*

The weapon—when it was finally released—initially seemed harmless. Almost gentle. All we heard was a light jangling sound, like countless needle points clattering a hard surface. Spreading in a wide spectrum from the edges of my mouth, the points were nearly silent at first, not scary at all, just individual metallic *clicks*. But gradually they grew in volume, and before long people were shrieking as the noise mounted into a broad and deafening accelerando.

This is the danger note, I realized. *I have to stop the clicks.*

Please, I thought. *Please. Stop. Please.* I kept telling my throat that. Kept telling it there was no danger. And it was beginning to react to my wish. I was finally starting to gain a basic level of control over the noises, to shut

118

them down. If Nina had touched me just a few seconds later, I might have been able to prevent what happened.

It wasn't her fault. She was only trying to hold the noises back. Her face was pointed away from mine, one of her hands fumbling for my lips. She did it in the same instinctive way she might have for a stereo blasting out. She only wanted to turn the volume down.

I saw what happened next, but was unable to prevent it.

First one of my arms launched out, intercepting Nina's wrist. Then, joining in that purpose, my tongue altered position, becoming a funnel that targeted her hand. "No!" I screamed, and at least I was able to stop my arm from killing her. But next second there passed through my lips a high-pitched *slit* of sound unlike anything that had come before. It emerged scarily fast and focused on the part of Nina that had made contact with me—her right forefinger.

Nina wore a plain platinum-plated ring on that finger, a present I'd given her on her fourteenth birthday. I could visualize precisely what was about to happen to that ring long before it occurred. It was going to be removed. It was going to be severed, along with the rest of the finger it was attached to. And then, while the ring and finger were still in midair, the clicks in my throat would vaporize them, destroying every last trace of the threat.

No, I won't let that happen, I decided. *I won't.*

Jerking my head away, to stop it I did the only thing I could.

I changed the target. I made it the worst possible target for my weapon.

My own hand.

Instantly, when it identified the flesh as mine, my throat powered down. The tics ceased. The few which had already escaped my lips faded, their only damage being to sear the outer skin on my palm.

Seconds later, I suddenly regained control of my voice.

"Get out!" I screamed at everyone. "Get out! Get out!"

Nina didn't react. She didn't seem to know what had happened. She just kept staring at my reddening hand, pawing at me softly, brokenly, an expression of disbelief on her face.

I surveyed the room. The noises had ended, but everyone was still terrified. The green-eyed boy was a wailing ball of fear. A mother was screaming. At the back of the room a juddering little girl was trying to cover her sister's bleeding ears.

To protect her and everyone else I had to get out. Clawing my way towards the front entrance, I stood and started running. The last thing I saw before I left the café was the owner holding Nina upright while he banged out an emergency call on his mobile.

17

Mammals. The pinnacle of evolution on Earth. Deadly, intelligent, and superbly efficient.

The end of the dinosaur era opened the way for the earliest of them to roam and scurry, and as soon as the Ocrassa came across its first primitive rat, it knew it had hit upon a species spectacularly different from anything that had lived before.

Rooting inside the rat's brain, the Ocrassa found that nature had not retired from the contest. On the contrary, it had been quietly fashioning a more versatile weapon. The rat was smart. It could contemplate and plan. If nature ever created an opponent capable of challenging the Ocrassa, clearly the mammalian branch of evolution would provide it.

Over time, as the line of more advanced mammals began to appear—cats, dogs, whales—the Ocrassa made a point of examining each in turn and testing their strengths.

It could not, however, detect all the mammals.

And with one of them—wave-beautiful and packed with potential—nature surprised it.

The Ocrassa was in a shallow cold sea, ingesting krill, when a pod of ninety dolphins approached it from above. The dolphins blasted it with a new weapon—sonar. Sharp clicks of sound coming so fast and from so many sources destroyed the Ocrassa's sensitive ear drums. At the same time, the dolphins' submarine-like bodies struck the Ocrassa, ramming its gills and other exposed areas.

In response the Ocrassa activated its entire arsenal of defenses, tearing into the dolphins, but by the time it had killed them all its left side was temporarily paralyzed.

Shocked, the Ocrassa hauled itself back to land. It had not anticipated this weapon. By using sound to attack it, nature had come up with something entirely new. For as long as it could remember the Ocrassa had not feared for its life, but it did now. Where would the next attack come from? And was there also a land-based threat it had missed? Something being prepared for it secretly by nature?

A combination of traits?

An ultimate weapon?

For thousands of years afterwards the Ocrassa was extraordinarily careful. It switched to remoter lairs. It found new ways to hunt as well, and new ways to stay alert. And when it could no longer remember a time when it had been truly hungry it deliberately starved itself to remind itself what it was like to die.

It would never be complacent again.

18

I ran from the café. I rushed headlong, always into quieter streets, seeking emptiness.

I only stopped when I reached the locked gates of Greenwich Park. Jumping over them, I made straight for the shelter of the trees. Above me, the huge body of leaves was gone, but a stiff wind still gusted, snapping wisps of oak and birch against my face. The rooks in the treetops were all shrieking as well. I had no idea what they wanted from me, and I covered my ears.

My hand was burned, but not badly. My throat was back to normal as well, but my jaw still tingled from my barely averted attack on Nina. I ran from that. Ran from what I'd almost done to her. Was this the precious object I'd been guarding all this time? A weapon that struck out at anyone who came close. Attacked the people I most loved.

Bending over a tree stump I retched over and over, wanting the night to swallow me up. I didn't care about protecting what was in my throat anymore. Not even if I needed it to destroy a monster.

What difference did that make if I was a monster?

I might have killed Nina. The truth of that howled through me. And the worst thing was that she'd warned me this might happen.

Time to cut it out, I thought. *Time to get rid of it.*

I nearly rang Reece before making that decision. More than anything else I wanted his reassurance and advice about what to do. But I knew he would only try to talk me out of it, and I couldn't let him do that.

I checked the address book on my mobile. Professor Oliver Wicken's number was there, sent through yesterday by Annette in the hope that I would ring him. Trusting him as much as I trusted anyone, I rang it.

"Hello?"

"It's Savannah Grey."

"Savannah?" He sounded relieved. "I've been endeavoring to get hold of you through your guardian. Legally, I can't contact you directly, and—"

"There's something growing in my throat."

A pause. "What is it?"

"I don't know, but I want it cut out."

"Are you having trouble breathing?"

"No. But look at this." I sent the photo of my throat mobile-to-mobile. I didn't tell him about the episode at the café. I knew he wouldn't believe me, and it might also delay the operation if he thought I was in an unbalanced state of mind. The photo itself, of course, was enough to convince him to see me.

"What's your closest hospital?" he asked.

"Yours. I want it done there. I want you to arrange it. I don't trust anyone else. Will you take it out tonight if I come to King's?"

He hesitated. "I can arrange for it to be looked at, in any case. And I can be there to advise."

"OK, I'm coming in. You'll need to find a way to tie my arms down," I said.

"We can't forcibly restrain you," Olly objected. "And you realize I won't be able to do anything without the written consent of your guardian."

"I'll get that for you."

I hung up and rang Nina.

"Sav?" She groaned. "Your hand—"

"It's OK," I said quickly, holding back my tears. "Listen to me, I'm not sure I can trust my voice. Not even to talk to you down the phone. But I'm going to King's. I'm getting it cut out, Nina. By the time I see you again it'll be gone. I'm going right now."

Ending the call to her, I ran from the park. I ran effortlessly, just like at Battersea. I was also aware of thinking exceptionally fast again. Quick, precise thoughts. Good. Now I'd made up my mind, that could only help me carry out what I had to do.

Reaching home, I told a shocked Annette what I'd agreed with Olly. She didn't need much convincing once I showed her the throat photo. Shoving her purse into her bag, she grimly got into the car and drove us both to King's. I sat in the backseat, keeping my lips shut. All that mattered was getting to the hospital quickly and without harming anyone. I was terrified of losing control of my throat again.

We hit traffic on the journey. Annette also wanted to talk, but I shook my head to show her I couldn't.

When we arrived Olly was waiting just inside the automatic sliding doors of the emergency-room entrance. He radiated both concern and reassurance—exactly what I needed in that moment—and escorted us straight to his office. I half-feared Carol Edilman would be there, but of course like any sensible person she was keeping well away from me.

Switching on his desk light, Olly asked me to sit down, angling an overhead strip lamp towards my face.

"It's OK," I told him, when he hesitated to approach. "Just don't get too close." During the car ride this had been my main focus—working out how to keep my throat in check if anyone came near my mouth. I let Olly shine his torch inside my lips. It was agonizing, but since the attack in the café I seemed to have more control, and I managed it.

For a moment Olly wavered in making his decision. Then something *fluttered* in my throat.

It was the only time I ever heard Olly swear.

Annette's eyes widened when she heard the noise as well, and she immediately signed the consent form for surgery.

Olly called a throat specialist into his office—the man who would perform the operation. I let him check inside my mouth. It was almost unbearably hard, coming so soon after Olly, but I hid my distress. I knew I had to. I didn't want anything giving them doubts about going ahead.

By the time he'd finished poking around, I was drenched in sweat. Once or twice a *click* discharged from my throat, but not loud enough for either man to hear. I was aware of the warning symptoms now, and suppressed the sounds as soon as they emerged. I had to keep doing this, minute by minute. It was incredibly difficult because, invaded this way, my throat wanted to disable, maybe kill, both men. I didn't tell them this. I knew that they would only cancel the operation and probably call the police. *I have to get rid of it*, I thought. *I have to.*

After consulting privately with the throat specialist, Olly checked a form. "Have you had anything to eat or drink in the last four hours?"

"No," I told him truthfully.

"OK," he said. "Here's what's going to happen. I've already alerted on-call surgical staff to prep an OR. Having seen with my colleague what's in your throat—whatever it is—I regard it as a potential risk to your life, and hence it constitutes an emergency. Mrs. Coombs agrees."

I nodded. I wanted him to hurry up and get on with it. It wasn't easy keeping the noises at bay.

"We can't restrain you physically," Olly said, as if the very idea repelled him. "It's not hospital policy."

"You have to find a way to hold down my arms," I told him. I had something heavy-duty in mind, like the industrial-strength straps you see on lorries for tying down cargo loads. Olly thought I was joking when I mentioned them. He was out of his comfort zone here. Annette, taking her lead from me this time, backed me up, but Olly wasn't happy.

"We'll tie you down if we have to," he said finally. "Savannah, I want you to understand exactly what we're going to do. The operation involves making an incision in your neck. We'll look to see what's in there, and if necessary—and only if necessary—remove it. Performing the operation requires us to use what we call a neuromuscular blocking agent. This temporarily paralyzes all the muscles in your body. So that you can still take in air, an oxygen tube is inserted through your nose so a machine can breathe for you."

"OK." I chose that one word carefully. I wanted to keep my lips tight shut. Didn't they understand how hard it was for me having them this close?

"The paralyzing agent has the added advantage . . . that we won't get any distractions from other parts of your anatomy," Olly noted. He glanced at my arms.

"She won't feel anything, will she?" Annette asked, holding my hand. "No pain?"

"None," Olly told her. "We'll use a general anesthetic." He turned back to me. "I expect the throat incision to be no more than two to three centimeters in diameter. The cut will fade somewhat over time. Do you understand everything I've told you?"

"Yes."

"Mrs. Coombs, do you have any further questions?"

"Can her friend stay with her?"

I looked up in surprise. Annette was smiling down at me. "Nina's been waiting outside to see you," she said. "I'll stay here at the hospital, but I thought you'd prefer her at your bedside while they get you ready for surgery."

"Thank you," I whispered, so grateful. "Thank you."

Annette moved behind me and Nina timidly made her way into Olly's office.

"You . . . you don't have to do this," I stumbled. "Nina, you don't have to be here. You don't have to stay with me. It's OK . . ."

"I'm not going anywhere," she said. "I've got to make sure you get rid of it, haven't I?" She managed a tight-lipped smile.

"I *am* going to get it cut out," I told her.

"You promise?"

I nodded fervently.

"Nina can remain with you until we take you down to the anesthetic room," Olly explained, before leaving with the throat specialist.

I could see that Nina was desperate to talk about events in Alfredo's, but I mouthed *I can't* and all it took was a single flutter from my throat to keep her as silent and focused as I was.

A slim nurse with a thick African accent prepared me for surgery. I was handed a skin disinfectant solution to wash my neck and a thin blue hospital gown. It was awkward to tie as I had to reach behind me. Nina helped, joking that I'd put on weight.

The nurse asked if I was wearing any metal jewelry or piercings. Nina told her no, she never wears stuff like that, but the nurse checked my hands, wrists, and neck to be sure. With Nina doing most of the talking I kept my answers brief, and very soon after that the nurse was accompanying me as I was wheeled down to surgery.

Nina forgot she couldn't come with me. She was still gripping the sides of the gurney when it reached the door leading to the surgical area. The nurse said something, and Nina suddenly understood she had to stay behind, and her eyes met mine.

"You're going to be OK," she said fiercely, holding my gaze. "You are. You know that, don't you?"

I nodded, holding back tears, not wanting to be left alone.

"It's OK, Sav," Nina whispered. "You're gonna get it out now. You are. It'll be gone ... be completely gone ..."

I reached for her hand. I wasn't scared to touch it in that moment. My throat had no fear of Nina, only of what was to come.

"I'll be here, waiting," she murmured. "You'll be fine. You will." She fervently kissed my hand, despite the risk, and mouthed *I love you.* And then there was no time to say anything else because I was being whisked through heavy double doors.

At a separate, enclosed room I was met again by Olly and the anesthetist.

"I'll be attending the operation myself," Olly said.

I was relieved and nodded, still thinking of Nina.

"After the operation you'll wake up in a special recovery room," Olly explained. "It's possible you'll still have one or two tubes in your mouth and nose when you come around, so don't be alarmed if you find them there."

"OK."

"You'll feel uncomfortable when you wake as well," he warned me. "Woozy. Dry-mouthed. Very disoriented. And it'll be difficult swallowing, I'm afraid."

"Can you make sure Nina's there when I wake up?"

"Yes, I'll do that." He gave me a genuinely reassuring smile.

"OK. I'm ready."

I attempted a smile of my own, but it fell flat.

Olly backed away and the anesthetist suddenly loomed over me. It came as a shock because he did so without warning, and it was all I could do to hold my throat in check. I didn't tell him that, though. He already looked worried. If he'd heard about Carol Edilman—which no doubt he had—he was probably nervous enough. To keep myself focused while he did his last checks, I concentrated as hard as I could on what I'd nearly done to Nina. I pictured a fingerless hand, fixing it in my mind.

Looking up from the gurney at the anesthetist's bearded chin, I think this was the first moment I truly began to believe that I might be able to go through this. I was as ready as I could be. I'd prepared myself. I'd kept my throat under control. And the best part was the anesthetic. If I could get as far as that, the drugs would leave me unconscious long before they prodded anything near my mouth.

For a moment I thought of Reece, and wished more than anything that he was here with me. But it was too late for that. In any case, I didn't want to risk any last-second doubts. My own mind was giving me enough of those, screaming for me to stop. But it had been doing that ever since I rang Olly, and I ignored it now just as I'd ignored it on the journey here.

I lay flat on the gurney and the anesthetist inserted a cannula into my wrist. This is it, I thought. I blinked, knowing how dangerous the next few moments would be. If my throat was going to make a final attempt to stop the operation, it was now. Why were they waiting so long to strap down my arms?

The anesthetist injected a milky-looking substance into the cannula. It gave me a slightly floaty feeling. "When are you going to tie me down?" I growled at Olly. "It can't wait! You need to do it now."

He smiled. "Count down from ten."

"Why?"

"Just count."

I blinked at him. "You're not going to strap down my arms, are you?" I realized. "You . . . you've just given me the anesthetic. . . ."

My mind was already blanking out. Relief flooded me, and I couldn't help thinking how clever it was of Olly to get around the problem that way. No danger from my throat if it didn't know what was happening to me. I was almost able to grin as I passed out—

—and woke again.

My eyes sprang open. I sat up. Simultaneously, I took in several things. One: I was on a surgical table. Two: my gown had been loosened to my waist. Three: clusters of intensely bright lights were shining in my eyes.

There was a handle in the middle of the lights.

My body took control at once—grasping the handle and shoving it aside.

Now I could now see more clearly. The walls were apple green. I was in an operating theater.

I was *still in* the operation.

My brain felt on fire, processing information extraordinarily fast. It was just like when I'd felt threatened at Battersea Park, only this time I was reacting even more quickly.

I'm in terrible danger, I realized.

As if to confirm it my eyes began fast-flickering, seeking the source of a low-level hum. To my left, there was some kind of breathing machine. Two tubes from the machine led to my nose. One of my own arms reached across, tore away the tape holding the tubes down to the sides of my nostrils, and hauled both of them out in one long and excruciatingly painful tug.

There was another, thinner, transparent tube attached to my wrist. As soon as I ripped this out, blood leaked from a vein. Some aspect of me evaluated the level of bleeding. It was bad, but not bad enough to kill me.

I continued to react incredibly fast. It was terrifying, but at the same time I sensed that my survival depended on it. I was aware of various emotions—fear, surprise, my intense feelings for Reece and Nina—only as something in the background of my mind.

Behind me there was a display monitor. Wires from it terminated in three patches on my body: one on each of my bare shoulders, the other against my belly.

I yanked them off.

I was no longer attached to anything.

Possessing freedom of movement, I swiveled to check for other threats. There was still a low electrical hum in the room. Where was it coming from?

The closest objects to me were bowls on carts. One contained a forceps dipped in brown liquid. It didn't look dangerous, so I moved on to the people. Olly was standing by the side of the bed, next to the anesthetist. Nearby, I recognized nurses and surgical staff from the team introduced to me earlier. I'd been moving so rapidly until this point that so far the only reactions I'd had from them were shocked expressions of disbelief.

I knew why I'd woken myself from the anesthetic. I'd counteracted the drugs pumped into me. Somehow my own body had found a way to neutralize them, kickstarting me back to consciousness before any damage could be done to my throat.

I remained frightened, but in my actions I was *precise*. I knew exactly what I needed to do next to survive. And for the first time I knew: *this is what you have to be like to kill a true monster. You need to be able to think this rapidly, this clinically, making instant, correct judgments.*

My eyes identified the source of the electrical hum. It came from a knife. The anesthetist was standing to the right of the bed, holding a blade towards my throat. It looked like a normal blade, but it wasn't. It was linked via wires to a machine.

An electric knife.

I felt my neck. Intact. They hadn't started yet.

Another second passed. During that time the anesthetist stepped away from the bed and all the other staff stared at me in frank amazement. It was Olly who got his nerve back first.

"It's OK," he whispered. "I can't explain this, but you must have been given the wrong anesthetic or not enough." He looked genuinely shaken. So did the others.

"No," I said. "I was given enough."

The knife was too close. I knocked it out of the anesthetist's hand. One of the nurses was trembling, and I welcomed that, not because I intended her any harm but because it meant she was less likely to be a threat. It was extraordinary how fast I was thinking and moving.

My eyes did a final sweep of the room for further risks, compromises, potential hazards. I saw none.

I swung off the table. Feeling dreadfully thirsty, I looked for water. There was a beaker of clear liquid at the side of the room.

"No, don't move, stay where you are," Olly warned me. "You could hurt yourself. I don't know what went wrong, but you're still partially sedated. It's unsafe for you to get up."

He was mistaken. I felt fresh and wide awake. I sniffed the beaker, made sure it was water, and drank it down in one swift gulp.

Was it safe outside the room? I didn't know. Being unsure about that, my priority was to get to a secure place as fast as possible. All this reasoning took place in an abstract way in my head. I assessed automatically. I was frightened, but it was a survival instinct, not fear, controlling my mind.

My immediate problem was practical. I needed to get out of the building, but underneath my thin hospital gown I was semi-naked. Plus it was night, so I'd be cold. My body could compensate for that, but it would waste energy I might need for another purpose. A simpler solution was in front of me. There was a sterile gown and matching trousers on a bench beside the tallest nurse. I asked her to hand over the clothes. She was too frightened to argue.

Blood still seeped from my wrist. Now that other threats had been eliminated or removed, I clamped a hand over the wound.

I was in pain, but I barely registered it. I blocked it out. It was irrelevant.

I stood up, throwing the remaining drapes off my upper body. Fastening the nurse's uniform around my back, I strode across the floor and sniffed another beaker of clear liquid. Water again. I drank it down, never taking my eyes off the people in the room.

Olly was repeating his message about it being dangerous to move around. He was wrong. My muscles had a fluid, supple ease he'd never know.

"I need a mobile phone," I said.

"Your possessions ... aren't here," the anesthetist stuttered.

"I know that. Anyone's will do."

The anesthetist glanced at Olly.

I didn't have time to wait for their slow decision-making. I needed a mobile to provide me with options when I left.

My arm shot towards the anesthetist so fast that he didn't see it until it was against his chest. I didn't hurt him, but he got the message and hurriedly fetched his own mobile from a side room.

Pocketing the phone, I left the operating theater, heading up the corridor. My eyes read all the signs around me quickly and efficiently. I exited by the shortest route. A security guard at the door saw me flash by, but I ran past him before he could stop me. Even if he'd wanted to stop me, he couldn't have.

Outside, darkness enveloped me. My eyes immediately compensated, using every scrap of available light to choose a path. There was vegetation to my left: a small municipal area, grass and scrub. Vaulting the fence leading to it, I headed for the nearest trees.

19

The Ocrassa waited for a new opponent to emerge from the mammals, but none came. Whatever nature was working on, it kept the secret to itself. Brooding within one of its temporary lairs, the Ocrassa decided it needed a defender to watch over and guard it. But where to find such a thing? Even if it could train some of nature's predators to do its bidding, the Ocrassa realized that it could never trust them not to turn against it.

Time, then, to create a life-form of its own.

The Ocrassa had learned a great deal about how creatures bred over its long existence. The main problem was how to blend different species to produce a distinctive new animal that obeyed it.

It began cautiously. Taking eggs and sperm from numerous animals, it variously combined and ripened them. The resultant birth-things never lived for long, but one or two had lungs and cried before they died. The Ocrassa watched their last hours, fascinated.

Gradually, over time, it was more successful. A snake-frog combination expired almost immediately, but its long, skinny body hopped once first. An ox-leopard loped confusedly around for six whole days, its brain wanting to hunt meat, its stomach desiring grass. The Ocrassa drowned it without a thought, but learned from it and began afresh.

After centuries, it managed to combine the intelligence of a pig and a dog into a workable unity. The fusion was smart and fiercely loyal, and could be trained to hunt. But best of all, when the Ocrassa created a second one, it could breed.

Once it was satisfied the template was good enough, the Ocrassa bred the pig-dogs in large numbers, posted them surreptitiously around its lairs and sent them in forays to look for nature's traps. The pig-dogs were trustworthy, enjoyed their work, and each one was dedicated to its master.

But the Ocrassa still felt vulnerable. It needed a more personal defender at its side. Something large enough to deter any predator, but also shrewd enough to be able to act alone if needed.

It required every scrap of the Ocrassa's prodigious understanding of life and nature to create the master-piece that followed. More than a thousand years of trial and error were needed to perfect the body, ten times that to design the brain.

When it was finally ready, the Ocrassa blew anxiously on its creation to dry it out and inflate its lungs. The creature lay for a time wreathed in a bed of twigs, learning how to breathe. All living things, no matter what they will become, must first learn how to breathe.

It was two meters wide. Standing erect on its bipedal legs, it was nine meters tall. The legs were thick haunches of meat, massively powerful, but the hollow, thin-walled bones made it deceptively fleet when running. The body was a tour de force of camouflage: part fur, part skin. The creature was able to change color at will. It could shade to grey areas, hide in small niches, disappear. At night, unless it wanted to be seen, it was undetectable.

The muscular arms were sinuous, ending in retractable claws. For the head, the Ocrassa delved into its memory. The result was a noble throwback to the great voracious reptiles of the Jurassic.

Lavishing attention on its new defender, the Ocrassa gave it everything it might need. Because they help clear the eyes, it even gave it tear ducts. But most of all the Ocrassa paid attention to the creature's brain. Much more than the pig-dogs, this creature could think for itself.

The Ocrassa concentrated on obedience training. It also built centers in the creature's mind that emphasized self-protection. After all the effort that had gone into its construction, the last thing the Ocrassa wanted to risk was that its new creation killed itself—accidentally or deliberately.

From the moment it was born the creature learned fast. Praise and rebuke enlivened it, but in truth it responded to everything. Like all intelligent animals, its tastes and inclinations were unique. It preferred cold weather to warm. Enjoyed showers but not heavy rain.

It was afraid of its first snowfall.

The Ocrassa laughed, seeing that.

It had given the creature forward-facing eyes, like its own, and they stared at the Ocrassa with bright and willful curiosity. Initially the Ocrassa communicated through signs and gestures only, but the creature had vocal cords and was smart enough to develop language.

Endearingly anxious to please its master, the creature improved itself. One day, spontaneously, it took over the management of the pig-dogs. And finally the Ocrassa knew it was ready to assume its duties, because it asked for something.

A name.

The Ocrassa gave this some thought.

"You are a night shape, a killer," said the Ocrassa in its own language. "A figment and framing of terror."

It named it *The Nyktomorph.*

20

It was dark around me—no stars or moon—and well past midnight. Like some kind of feral animal I'd taken cover behind a patch of trees, wrapping their soft, leafy branches around my shoulders to make me feel safer.

It didn't make me feel safer.

I only slowly eased down from the heightened aware-ness of the operating room. Glancing down at my wrist, I saw that the bleeding had almost stopped—and the minor burn I'd given myself at Alfredo's was gone altogether.

So I heal quickly as well.

Shuddering, unable to bear the thought of being out here on my own anymore, I desperately wanted Reece with me. I needed him. We were supposed to be in this together, but all I'd done was leave him unprotected. He couldn't even reach me if he was in trouble.

Was he?

Armed only with the anesthetist's mobile, it took me several fumbled attempts to remember his number correctly, but at last I heard his voice.

"Hello?"

"It's me," I burst out. "Can you talk?"

"Not really," he said. "Dad's in trouble. He had another attack while we were having dinner at home." Reece's voice was hushed. "The ambulance got to us in time, but it's not looking good. I'm with him now at King's. You sound like you're outside. Are you OK?"

I explained about the café and the failed operation, and we agreed to meet at the Lonsdale Ward, where his dad was being treated.

On the way I phoned Annette—she'd gone home, thinking I'd end up there—to tell her I was safe. I thought about ringing Nina too, but after promising to go through with the operation what was I supposed to say to her?

It started raining on the journey back to King's, and by the time I arrived my blue hospital gowns were soaked through.

Standing inside the main entrance, waiting for me, of course, was Nina.

"I tried to go through with it," I faltered. "I did. I—"

"You're alive," she whispered.

"Alive? Of course I'm al . . ." But she hadn't known that, had she? Olly had reported me running away, pumped full of chemicals. While I'd crouched in the scrub and grass, Nina had been frantically looking for me across the hospital grounds, expecting at any second to come across my unconscious or dead body.

She stood there shivering, her trousers spattered with mud.

"Oh, Nina," I murmured. "Oh, Nina . . . I am so sorry. . . ."

I tentatively reached out for one of her hands. After hearing from Olly, I could tell she was scared to be so close to me, but after making sure she'd know it was safe I held her tentatively, feeling her warmth through my cold gown.

In a private corner, Nina helped me change out of my sodden clothes. I've no idea how she'd managed it, but by borrowing or stealing she'd somehow come up with a shirt, jeans, and flat shoes roughly my size. As we toweled off we kept looking at each other. Between those looks, Nina tried to wipe the mud off her trousers, but she was shaking too much. She kept spreading the dirt higher up the hems. Seeing that, all I wanted to do was take her away from all of this, get her as far from danger as I could, somewhere safe. But first I needed to talk to Reece, and she agreed.

Mr. Gandolfo's bed was next to a bay window overlooking the largest hospital car park. The lights in the ward were dimmed, and by the time Nina and I got there, most of the patients, including Mr. Gandolfo, were asleep.

Reece was asleep as well. He lay slumped in an uncomfortable-looking chair. He looked exhausted, but hearing me approach he stood up and smiled. It was the sort of unreserved smile in other circumstances I'd have kissed him for.

"How is he?" I murmured, pulling up a stool near his dad's bed.

"Peaceful for now," he said. "You should have seen him earlier, though. The doctors had to sedate him. He keeps yelling. Pointing outside as if he can see something."

"Was it another stroke?"

Reece nodded, bowing his head. "The worst yet. The doctors say . . . he'll probably never walk again."

Not wanting to wake his poor dad, Nina quietly pulled up a chair and the three of us spoke in whispers, going over what had happened during the operation. "Even while you were under the anesthetic your body sensed you were in danger and woke you," Reece marveled. "Incredible." He was fascinated by all the details, but at some point he stopped asking questions, and said, "You must have been scared to death."

His fingers brushed my knee, and I nodded, reveling in even that fleeting touch.

"You really believe *you're* the monster now, don't you?" he murmured.

"Aren't I?" I said, unable to meet his eye. "You were there while McCarthy did his tests. Look at these hands." I lifted them. "I could break anyone's head open with these. Even if someone knew I was going to do it, they couldn't stop me."

Reece's palm was still on my knee. "But you wouldn't use them against anyone. That's the difference."

"I hurt that doctor at the hospital," I said. "I nearly hurt . . ." I glanced shamefully at Nina.

"But you didn't," Reece said, and Nina nodded firmly.

"But I *might* have!" I said angrily. "I can't get rid of what's in my throat. Whatever's in there won't allow me. I can't bear this. All I want . . . I just want . . ." I was about to say *to be a normal girl again*, but I didn't. What was the point in even wishing for that now? Because if one thing was obvious, it was that I needed all these extra abilities. Something horrifying was out there. What else could explain my frightening gifts? And while Nina and Reece seemed to think that the star-headed creature was the only monster after us, I wasn't so sure. It seemed unlikely all these gifts were needed just to face that dog-thing. More likely *another* monster was out there. Something we hadn't seen yet.

Something worse.

I could see Nina searching for words to comfort me, but she couldn't find them. How could anyone find them? In that moment, there was only one question that mattered to me.

"Are we still human, Reece?"

He looked up sharply. "Of course we are. But did you really think our bodies could stay as they were to fight what's waiting for us out there? You're not a monster,

Sav," he said fervently. "I don't think monsters worry about their humanity. I don't think they get concerned they're becoming too human."

He lifted my chin, made me look at him. "You think a monster likes this?" he said, running his fingers through my hair. "Or has any feelings when someone does this?" He stroked my shoulder, all the way down my arm. "You think a monster would even notice what we're feeling? Or care if they did?"

Reece was still holding my arm when his dad suddenly woke and sat up in bed.

The first thing I noticed was how harshly twisted Mr. Gandolfo's face was from the latest stroke. He turned towards a passing orderly—no interest—then Nina—no interest—and finally me. As soon as he recognized me he became agitated.

"I s-saw it!" he blurted, one arm dangling uselessly by his waist.

"Shush, Dad, it's OK," Reece whispered gently.

Mr. Gandolfo ignored him. Fumbling at the window, his nose banged off the frame. "It's still . . . still . . . there!" he choked, his breath misting the glass.

"Dad, look at me," Reece said. "There's nothing outside. You're safe. You're in hospital, remember?" He folded the blankets back over his father's legs, and Nina joined in the effort to calm him down.

But Mr. Gandolfo would not be calmed. He peered from the window again, and this time whatever he saw or thought he saw made him whimper with fear. A spasm of pain crossed his face—some after-effect of the stroke—but it didn't distract him. Whatever he was seeing outside was more important.

I followed his stare into the poorly lit car park. At first I saw nothing except a handful of vehicles in the front bays. Then my eyes started fast-flickering.

Mr. Gandolfo managed to stand up, waving wildly at the window.

Reece said, "Dad, please sit down. You'll hurt yourself."

"Let him talk," I said. "Let him speak."

"It . . . it . . . it . . . came to the house," Mr. Gandolfo stuttered. It cost him an enormous amount just to get those short words out. His concentration was terrifying. "Our faces . . . were th-th-this far apart." He pinched a tiny gap between his fingers. "*A monster*. It asked about . . . about my boy"—he brushed Reece's face warmly with his quavering fingers. "It . . . it could *talk*."

Heaving for breath, Mr. Gandolfo's hand flapped for a glass of water. Reece made him lie down again and helped him sip from it. Everyone waited for more, but the words had dried up.

A ward nurse scuttled up to us, to see if she was needed. While Reece spoke to her, I checked the rear of the car park, my eyes on the shaded areas between the cars.

And suddenly all the hairs rose up on my scalp.

"Something's out there," I said.

Mr. Gandolfo nodded dramatically. "Yes . . . yes." Tears of gratitude sprang up in his eyes. "You . . . s-s-see it?"

"I don't see anything," Nina murmured. She squinted out of the window, shaking her head. "It's empty, Sav. There's nothing out there."

"No," I said. "It's bigger than the cars."

The monster—camouflaged, and more than four times my height—was leaning casually against one of the parking meters. Without my improved eyesight I'd have assumed it was only a dappled shadow, the outline was so indistinct. For Mr. Gandolfo to have spotted it, I knew he must have known exactly what to look for. He must, in other words, have seen it before.

It *had* visited him.

"Where?" Reece craned his neck.

I briefly lost the monster in the shadows. Then I caught a hint of its head shape: reptilian, recessed oval eyes under heavy brows.

As I ran to the window, those eyes glanced up and met mine. The monster did not flinch or look away. It gazed steadily at me, as if waiting to be noticed. Its body was a mosaic of fur patches alternating with puckered bare flesh. The skin arrangement reflected the surroundings, seamlessly blending in.

A huge surge of fear shot through my body at its sheer size, and I drew back from the window, trying to decide what to do. The monster was hardly outside by accident. I'd been too scared to chase the star-headed creature when I first saw it. Was I going to let fear stop me following this one as well? But we had to know why they were stalking us. . . .

"Don't go out there," Nina rasped, as if she was reading my thoughts.

I hesitated. With panic tumbling in great waves up and down inside me, I gazed out again at the reptile. Then, forcing myself to move, I brought my fist down, smashing the window lock.

The second floor was over forty feet above the ground. I clambered out onto the narrow ledge.

"Sav!" Nina yelled, trying to pull me back.

I held her off gently. I checked the distance to the ground. Would my spine take the impact from this height? It was tempting to go the easier route—via the stairs—but if I went that way I'd lose sight of the monster, and it might get away.

"Don't come after me," I warned, turning to both Reece and Nina. "Stay here. Protect each other."

I sprang from the window. While I was still in midair the monster's eyes locked on mine. It didn't look afraid. It looked, in fact, as if it was waiting for me. It was only when I hit the paved area in front of the Golden Jubilee wing—landing safely between two parked cars—that it started to run.

21

The monster was clearly built for speed. On agile, three-toed feet it leapt effortlessly over the car park's brick wall. Then, without pause, it leapt again, this time landing a huge distance down Bessemer Road.

Its body crunched into a parked Renault van. The impact was so solid it demolished the vehicle's entire left side, and my first thought was that the monster had panicked and struck the vehicle by mistake. But then I saw the way it used the mass of the van to ricochet further up the street. Uninjured, it briefly passed in front of three dark-green bins, its color merging with theirs. Then it eased up another street, and I realized that if I didn't go after it now I'd never catch it.

I doubted I could match the speed of anything that moved so fast, but within seconds I was beyond the car park, onto the path and following the monster across Venetian Road.

Even so, I barely kept pace. My only advantage was that as it picked its way across the streets, its sheer bulk left clues in its wake: branches swaying, litter flattened.

I caught a glimpse as it leapt a shuttered gate leading to a construction site.

Moments later, I vaulted the same fence.

The site was enclosed. On three sides were high walls, maybe ten meters tall. The only way out was back over the gate, towards me. Since there were no other exits the monster had to be inside, but I couldn't see it.

Where was it hiding?

The yard was a typical construction site. A stack of haphazardly piled steel girders caught my attention. The girders looked innocent enough—surely something the size of the monster couldn't hide behind them?—but I decided to make sure.

I was no more than a body length away from the piled-up steel when there was . . . activity.

The girders stirred—and parted.

I stepped back in shock. All this time the camouflaged monster had been sitting nonchalantly on the steel, in plain sight, simply watching me. If it hadn't moved, even with my improved vision I'd never have seen it.

So why had it moved? *Because it wants me to see it?* That was a frightening thought, and I retreated until my back was near the gate.

Standing up to its full height—dwarfing the walls— the creature gazed down at me. I searched for any fear in its heavily lidded eyes, but saw none. On the contrary it stared candidly at me, and the realization came: *it wants me to see it. It wants me to* assess *how dangerous it is.*

The monster's face was fully reptilian and covered in cuts and burns. Long-healed burns. Dozens of them, especially under its eyes, as if its head had been caught in a fire.

"What do you want?" I yelled.

No answer.

"What are you doing here?"

The monster simply stood there, poised. It didn't look alarmed. Even if it was, how could I tell? Would it cry out in fear? Somehow I doubted it.

A light rain was falling, droplets glistening off the monster's skin and fur. Trembling, not sure what else to do, I stood my ground. For a moment the monster studied me. Then it lifted its arms up above its immense shoulders, showing me the knifelike serrations running along their edges. And then, even more slowly, to command my attention—which it did—it opened its vast, clawed hands.

It's showing me it has no concealed weapons.

I now understood, if I'd been in any doubt before, that this was no dumb brute responding to basic fight-or-flight instincts. It was intelligent, and all I could do was wait with a terrible throb of fear for what it might do next.

"You can speak, can't you?" I challenged it. "You talked to Mr. Gandolfo."

No answer.

"My name is Savannah Grey. *What are you?*"

Again no reply, but at the mention of my name the monster tilted its head on one side.

"Do you have a name?" I whispered. The prospect that this creature might have anything as human as a name was somehow even more frightening than its appearance. If it had one, I didn't want to hear it.

"I am the Nyktomorph."

The words came out in a hauntingly low voice, nasal but clear. Then, dismissing the notion that it was in any way human, the monster—the Nyktomorph—threw back its head and roared.

The roar blasted across the yard, flashing off the walls.

As the sound receded, the Nyktomorph reached up. Making sure I was watching, it slowly raked its claws across its throat, as if to say to me, *I will do this to you.*

That was when I saw the object attached to the left side of its body. Something I'd ignored as a piece of dead or flapping skin was actually . . . another separate and living monster.

The star-headed creature.

Oh God, there are two of them.

Trying to guess how much danger I was in, I backed off.

The star-headed creature took that as its cue to scuttle down the Nyktomorph's flank. Its body was roughly the shape of an oversized dog, but nothing else about it was remotely canine. Its spectacular head was formed by five star-prongs, for a start. Sunk inside the upper three prongs, constantly blinking, was a lone blue eye that was mobile, eager, and moist. Below that hung a black snout with tooth-filled lips.

The lips were covered in messy spatters of yellow liquid. Looking closely, I saw that the creature's entire body was covered in the stuff. It was the same yellow fluid I'd seen over at Reece's house, but the source was the last place I would have expected—the creature's own mouth. To avoid the liquid—to breathe freely—it had to keep its lips wide apart all the time.

The star-headed creature's body, even at this range, smelled strongly of oil, and as it approached me, muttering *pas pas*, using scary, dancelike steps, my gaze was drawn to its hair.

Or rather, its wig. The blond locks wrapped around its three upper prongs were definitely human. It wore a dress as well. A tattered yellow ballet dress, of all things—a tutu.

The garment was draped clumsily and inappropriately over its body. From the slashed look of the material, the owner had not given it up willingly.

The Nyktomorph gestured towards the star-headed creature, as if wanting to introduce it. Yes, that was exactly what it was doing.

"The Horror," announced the Nyktomorph.

It said the name tonelessly, like a statement of fact.

The Horror.

And watching the star-headed creature, the willful, hostile way it moved, I could believe it was.

Were they preparing to attack me? Impossible to tell. The Nyktomorph was all quiet contemplation and practiced stillness. The smaller monster gave the impression of being the opposite: fresh and damp and utterly wild.

And young. Why did I think that?

"I'll defend myself if I have to," I yelled, having no idea how I would do that. "Stay where you are!"

The Horror chortled and tugged at its own face. Then it gave the Nyktomorph a kiss on the side of the mouth. The frankness of that kiss made me gasp. Was this parent and child? But if the Horror was the offspring of the Nyktomorph, there was no resemblance.

What was I supposed to do? Keep talking to them? Threaten them? Neither had worked so far. The Horror in particular looked too wild to reason with. It was obvious from its rapid, unpredictable movements how untamed it was. It kept jumping towards me, then away again, as if this was an exciting game where the rules were being made up as we went along.

"What *are* you?" I demanded.

"What *are* you?" the Horror screamed back, copying my tone exactly. It grinned up at the Nyktomorph, seeking approval for the imitation. Then it approached me again, more speedily this time, dainty little steps full of menace on its suckerlike pads. Why did I get such a strong impression that it was a child?

"Keep away," I warned it, noisily striking the fence behind me.

"Keep away!" the Horror shouted back, bending to lick the ground.

Ignoring my warning, it approached me one prancing and yet eerily elegant step at a time. I backed off until the metal gate was firmly against my shoulder blades, and I had nowhere else to retreat.

"No!" I shouted, the way you might to scare off an aggressive dog.

"No!" the Horror repeated gleefully.

"Stay back! I mean it! I'll hurt you!"

"I'll hurt you!" The Horror fixed me with that incandescent, all-too-eager eye.

Then, astonishingly, it pirouetted. Followed by a small bow of its head—and, *hop*, *hop*, two dancelike somersaults.

Then I knew. It *is* a child. It's performing for me. This is some kind of trick it's learned. It wants me to notice it. It wants me to *approve*.

As if to confirm this, the Horror went through a full repertory of whirling ballet moves. Finally, barking "jeté," it ended up on one bent leg, rotating slowly.

Jeté sounded French to me, but the tone and voice used were young and female. Where had the Horror picked up that accent?

"Why are you here?" I demanded, my voice wavering.

The question was obviously meaningless to the Horror. It just kept performing full pirouettes, as if by doing them often enough I would take notice.

I blinked, incredulous. "You really *are* trying to impress me, aren't you?"

The Horror didn't understand, but I had the feeling the silent Nyktomorph did, and its interest in me deepened.

I turned from its silent scrutiny back to the Horror. Its claws were nearly close enough to snatch at me now. I couldn't allow that. I had to find a way to get its attention. Talk to it. Scare it. Or . . . would something else work?

Hardly able to believe what I was doing, I began making little *oooing* and *ahhing* noises. I used a nice soothing tone, the kind you might try on a baby to get its interest. The Horror was startled, but also . . . absurdly pleased. Its ears flicked up. It wriggled and clapped its tiny arms. Mewling *ahhhhh*, it licked its own face with delight.

The Nyktomorph nodded, as if it had been waiting for me to realize what I was dealing with. Then it uttered a guttural string of words. The words were aimed at the Horror, but whatever they meant the Horror didn't like them. It bared its teeth, wriggling the tiny, pointless-looking arms in the middle of its chest in frustration. The Nyktomorph merely growled louder, forcing it to listen.

Snarling with frustration, the Horror shook its star-points. Then, becoming childlike again, it cried to itself, tears pooling in its eye. I got the impression it had been told to leave me alone, when all it wanted to do was to carry on playing its threatening games.

The Nyktomorph soothed it into acceptance, using long strokes of its muscular claws to knead the Horror's face.

That seemed to work, and gradually the Horror calmed down, its twitching arms slowly coming to rest against the Nyktomorph's neck. But just when I thought the Horror was in a trance—or perhaps genuinely asleep—it jumped up again, and with a dramatic flourish scurried off.

Racing away unbelievably fast, with a yelp of fouetté it scaled the far wall of the yard, pouncing onto a nearby roof. For a moment it crouched there, cooing at me and mouthing exaggerated *ooooos* and *ahhhhhs*. Then it shot over a line of chimneys and was gone.

What was I supposed to do now? Follow the Horror? But I couldn't do that and also stay with the Nykto-morph. I decided to remain where I was. One reason was that even with my new speed I doubted I could keep up with the Horror. But there was another reason. I was still holding out the faint hope of communication with the Nyktomorph. This creature was definitely not a child.

Time passed and, silent and impassive, the Nykto-morph simply watched me with those calculating, hooded eyes. It had barely moved from its place beside the steel girders since I entered the yard. I had the scary feeling that it was controlling our encounter. Hadn't it traveled from the car park just fast enough for me to be able to follow? And it understood what I said as well. It had made that abundantly clear when it named itself.

But it hadn't spoken again. Why? Did it expect me to make the next move? Would it respond if I asked the right question?

"You were waiting for me, weren't you?" I said. "Waiting for me to turn up at the hospital."

No reply.

"Are there more of you?" I demanded. "More Nyktomorphs? More Horrors?"

Still nothing.

"Why did you run from the car park?"

Silence. We stood only a short distance apart, rain drizzling on our backs. I took a single step towards it.

"I know you can talk," I said. "If you can understand what I'm saying, show me."

This time the Nyktomorph nodded, though for the first time it trembled as well. Was it cold? Did something this big feel a chill?

"Why won't you answer my questions?"

No reply.

"Is it because you *can't* answer my questions?"

A gleam entered one of the Nyktomorph's eyes, and it nodded again. At the same time the trembling worsened. It looked under great strain, as if it wanted to talk but could not.

Does this creature have a master? I suddenly wondered, a freezing chill running through my blood. The monster from my dreams? Is that what this creature and the Horror obey?

"Have you been ordered not to say anything?" I yelled.

The Nyktomorph might have nodded again, but it was now trembling so much that I couldn't tell for sure.

"By what?" I demanded. "Who do you take your orders from?"

No response. Gradually the shaking of its body subsided and we both ended up standing quietly again, facing each other.

I wondered about the Nyktomorph's purpose in being here. Was it curious about me? Perhaps. Afraid of me? No, I didn't think it was afraid. And then the image of the Horror reentered my mind. I remembered the direction it had been heading as it sped over the rooftops.

"Back towards the hospital and Reece," I said out loud. "Is that what you're here for? To distract me? So the smaller one can get to him without me interfering?"

Something about the way the Nyktomorph went still and narrowed its eyes made me realize I was right.

I swiveled around.

The Nyktomorph reacted instantly, hurdling over my head until it stood on the other side of the gate.

I jumped to the top of the same gate, balancing there. How could I get past it? Would I have to fight? A complex expression passed across the Nyktomorph's face, as if it was also debating whether or not to stand in my way. When it did not—when it moved aside and let me go—I knew that it was not out of fear, but because no matter how fast my legs carried me back to the hospital I would be too late.

22

Reece and Nina were waiting together in the subdued light of the hospital ward when the Horror streaked across the car park. Scampering incredibly fast among the vehicles, it made no attempt to conceal itself. In truth, it didn't care who saw it. This time its task was simple, bloody, and direct, and it understood exactly what it had to do.

"What . . . is *that?*" Nina gasped.

The Horror hurdled Cutcombe Road and leapt onto the Golden Jubilee building. When it began climbing the glass-covered external walls, Nina slammed the window shut. Seeing that, the Horror hooted with mirth. It was already past the second floor, scaling its way up.

"Help me move my dad," Reece pleaded. "I don't think I can do it on my own."

"Wake him quick, then," Nina said, thinking with dread: *has Savannah had to fight that?*

Despite the urgency, it took Reece an age to rouse the groggy Mr. Gandolfo.

"We'll carry him between us," Nina said. "Come on! Come on!"

But before they could work out how to pick Mr. Gandolfo up, there was a noise at the window. A gentle *tap-tap-tap.*

The Horror was perched on the window ledge, gazing happily at them through the glass.

An elderly man in an adjoining bed saw it and his peal of fear woke everyone in the ward. Confusion followed as nurses, assuming the scream was related to a heart attack, set off the cardiac alarm. By the time the Horror smashed the window and leaned its star-head through, a doctor and two nurses had arrived.

The Horror was delighted to be the center of attention. Shaking its head from side to side, it merrily waved its vestigial arms at everyone, spattering yellow liquid all over the polished ward floor. One of the nurses slipped and fell on the liquid, immediately picked herself up again, and ran. Everyone else did the same, escaping any way they could.

Stepping through the broken window, a few quick, nimble steps took the Horror to the middle of the ward floor. There it posed and danced—flexing its belly, walking on its claws, slapping the floor. Then it shook its body and the yellow tutu dress, already hanging precariously from a shoulder, fell off altogether. The Horror grinned at its own nakedness and kicked the dress away.

Shouts echoed down the ward corridor as patients and staff fled. The Horror, enjoying itself immensely, pinched the patients slowest to reach the exits, gleefully repeating their cries.

Where's Savannah? Nina thought. *Has this smaller monster been sent to kill Reece while the big one she saw deals with her? I told her to get rid of what was in her throat,* she thought in dismay. *But I was wrong. She needed it, didn't she? She needed it to fight this.*

Mr. Gandolfo was still sleepy. He hadn't seen the Horror yet and was resisting Reece and Nina's efforts to lift him.

"Dad, please!" Reece begged.

The Horror paused to chew on a rubber sheet before ripping it to shreds.

Nina, barely containing her panic, realized that they had to get out now. If they didn't they'd be the last people left in the ward, and all the Horror's attention would be on them.

"We'll push the bed!" she told Reece.

She was about to get her weight behind the cumbersome metal frame when the Horror turned. No longer following the other patients, it looked straight at Reece—and swiveled to block his way.

"Get a weapon!" Reece whispered. "We have to threaten it somehow."

Nina glanced around for something large and solid, but there was nothing big to hand—just fruit, magazines, pillows, paper cups.

"The lamp on your side," Reece said. "Can you reach it?"

There was a desk lamp to Nina's left. She gripped it, but couldn't pass it to Reece—a cord tied it to a wall socket.

Mr. Gandolfo was at last fully awake. Seeing the Horror he shrieked and tried to get up, but couldn't coordinate his movements. Then he screamed again—some internal pain howling through him. The pain lifted him up and when he fell he hit the floor like a stone. Reece tried to get his hands under his shoulders to lift him back up.

The Horror shook its star-points at him.

"It's not after me or your dad," Nina realized. "Look! It doesn't even care whether we're here. See the way it keeps staring at you? What does it want?"

"I don't know," Reece said.

The Horror took a step towards him and waved a single curved claw at his throat.

"Oh no . . ." Reece protectively clutched the scar on his neck, backing off. The Horror followed him across the ward.

His throat, Nina thought. *It's like Savannah's. It wants to do something to whatever's inside.*

Without having much faith in the lamp, she picked it up, testing its weight. Even if she could use it, where was she supposed to hit the Horror? Its snout? Its eye? Then a terrifying thought flashed into her mind: *Is Savannah already dead? Has this thing killed her, and now come to kill Reece as well?*

"What do you want from me?" Reece shouted.

Almost all the nurses and other patients were now gone. A security officer arrived, skidding on his heels, but as soon as he saw the Horror he spun around again and left.

The Horror was irritated. It missed all the chaotic shouting and fleeing bodies. Briefly running from the ward, it hauled a nurse back inside. She shrieked as it pushed her against a wall and turned her face towards Reece.

It wants her to watch, Nina thought. *It wants an audience to see what it's going to do to him.*

The nurse lay slumped against the wall, not daring to move. The Horror made her open her eyes and patted her head—*a dog patting a human*, Nina couldn't help thinking. Then it scrambled up and down the walls of the ward, banging the ceiling with its claws, dripping and panting.

"Let's go!" Nina muttered to Reece, but before they could move the Horror was back. With a resounding thump on the floorboards, followed by an exultant shriek of "Entrechat!" it slammed all four feet down in front of Reece and bared its teeth.

Reece leaned back, shielding his neck.

Mr. Gandolfo had collapsed. He lay in a grey-faced heap on the floor, unmoving. The nurse stared numbly from the floor, her terrified eyes widening every time the Horror came anywhere near her.

It took all her nerve, but Nina stepped in front of Reece. The Horror, though, was uninterested in her. It moved in ever-tighter circles, gazing meaningfully at Reece's throat.

"Get me something to hit it with!" Reece begged. "Anything!"

Nina glanced around, but there was nothing big she could reach without leaving Reece exposed to the Horror. As it padded towards him, Reece did the only thing possible in the circumstances—he raised his fists. As if this was a universal signal even the Horror could understand, it rocked back on its hind legs and playfully wriggled its tiny arms, mocking him.

Holding her ground, Nina gripped and regripped the base of the lamp stand. It was awkward to hold. Worse, if the cord wasn't long enough she wouldn't be able to swing it. Scarily, the Horror's eye followed the cord and appeared to understand that.

"Can you push your dad away on the bed without my help?" she whispered to Reece.

"I'll try. What are you going to do?"

"I don't know." *Stay between you and it*, she thought.

Reece shoved his weight behind the bed. It was stiff, wouldn't budge.

"There's a brake on one of the wheels," Nina told him, never taking her eyes off the Horror. "You have to release it."

As Reece bent down to do so, the Horror lunged. It happened so fast that Nina knew all this time it had just been toying with them.

First, its teeth plucked the lamp stand from her hand. Then it rammed its snout into her belly, sending her sprawling across the ward. Swinging back to Reece, the Horror flipped him over onto his back. He struggled under it, but the Horror straddled his knees, holding him down with its weight. With Reece prone and looking up, the Horror smiled, seemingly content now to take its time. Its claws danced artistically in the air over his throat, as if this was a game it wanted to prolong for as long as possible.

Nina, winded from her fall, staggered back to Reece. The Horror didn't even turn around to deal with her this time. It whirled a free leg and struck her full in the chest, piling her against the back wall of the ward. She tried to get up again, failed. Her eyes desperately appealed across the room for help, but the nurse there could only watch, paralyzed by fear.

Reece was now entirely pinned down. With three of its legs, the Horror kept him that way. Its other leg played a little game of inching its way up his chest, towards his neck. When he resisted, the Horror raked its claws down his thighs, drawing blood, tearing through his shirt and jeans.

"No!" Reece screamed.

The Horror grinned. Closing its suckerlike hand into a fist, it punched him—rather delicately—on the nose.

The blow made Reece gasp and, while his mouth was open, the Horror slipped a large claw between his lips and stirred the contents of his throat. Humming softly to itself, little *ooos* and *ahhhhs*, it rummaged ever deeper clockwise and anticlockwise, probing, making incisions, finishing its task.

Then, without any fuss, it stepped back to assess its work.

Reece, letting out a terrible groan, slumped on his side, bringing his fingers up to cover his mouth.

The Horror pulled his fingers aside. It wanted to see what it had done.

Making sure, Nina thought, unable to rise from the floor.

A trickle of blood flowed from Reece's lips. But the contents leaking to the floor were not only blood-colored. They were honey-colored. They were chocolate-brown as well.

The Horror placed its star-face flat next to Reece's, to make sure everything important in his neck was gone. Following which, sighing contentedly, it sprang to the window ledge. For a few seconds it posed there, bowing as if it had given a masterly performance. Then, uttering a soft cry of "Ballon," it waggled its blond wig and scrambled off into the night.

But it came back. As if it had forgotten something, which it had, the Horror sheepishly reentered the ward. For a moment it twirled and preened itself in front of the nurse still lying against the wall. Then, plucking the shrieking Nina up, it dragged her a few feet across the floor, threw her like a sack over its bony shoulder, and leapt into the darkness.

23

By the time I made it back to the hospital, it was too late. Nina was gone, and Reece lay on an operating table in the Hambledon Wing surrounded by surgeons desperately trying to save his life.

"No, no, no," I screamed when I finally found him, but there was nothing I could do to help, so instead I tracked the Horror's yellow drips. The trail meandered all over the hospital grounds, giving me hope I'd be able to trace it to Nina, but eventually it just led me to a dead end in the middle of a section of grass. Within that grass, spelled out in a series of splattered drips—a deliberate taunt— was Nina's name.

Oh God, where is she?

Cursing myself, I pressed my thumbs bitingly hard into my cheekbones. Why had I stayed so long with the

Nyktomorph? Why hadn't I made sure Reece and Nina were hidden before I left them?

Running all around the hospital perimeter, my eyes searched everywhere for clues to where she might have been taken, but there were none, and finally all I could do was head back to Reece.

Somehow, startling the doctors with his will to live, he survived the operation. After it was finally over, he was transferred to the hospital's intensive care unit, where a nurse, taking pity on me, let me stay. I sat on a chair at the bottom of Reece's bed, and for hours I just watched him. Reece couldn't do anything for himself. A respiration tube breathed for him. Other devices fed him and got rid of waste. At one point he woke to discover a plastic pipe fixed to his mouth and it was horrifying to watch as he panicked, trying to pull it out. "I'm here, you're safe, don't move," I reassured him, but he must have been too disoriented to recognize me and his arms struggled to drag the tube out until the sedation drugs took him under again.

I should have hidden you, I thought, my head in my hands. *I should have hidden someone as precious as you.*

Annette didn't understand what was going on with me, but she did at least grasp that whatever it was, I needed to go through it alone, and I went home to get fresh clothes.

By dawn, when I returned to the ICU, Reece was finally conscious. Woozy and dazed-looking, he was being propped up against three pillows by a nurse. Seeing him, I rushed across. He spotted me over the nurse's head, and managed a faint smile, but the expression underneath it was desolate.

He couldn't talk directly to me—he still had a tube down his throat—but the police had given him a note-pad and a thick felt-tipped pen in case he remembered anything about the attack, and his hand was immediately scribbling.

What happened? Tell me everything.

I went over what I knew: Nina being kidnapped, meeting the Nyktomorph and Horror at the construction site. Reece listened intently, without interrupting, and when I finished wrote shakily on his pad:

What do you think the Horror will do to Nina?

I closed my eyes, thinking about the Horror's behavior at the building site. "It'll probably want to play," I whispered. "To be entertained." Reece looked appalled. "It's a child," I said. "More than anything else it likes fun and games."

And what if Nina refused to take part in those games? What would it do to her then?

Reece, seeing my stricken look, wrote:

Dad had been telling me about a monster visiting him for months. The words were garbled, but he got the message across. I just didn't listen.

"You couldn't have known what he meant," I said.

Reece reached angrily for his pad.

No, you don't understand. Every day he tried to tell me. Every single day.

Tears lined Reece's eyes. As they trickled down his face he swallowed, the pain clearly enormous. He was furious.

Dad's dead, he wrote. Everyone was too scared to come back into the ward until it was too late. They left him there on his own.

I tried to comfort him, but how could I? Reece had been readying himself for his dad's death for a long time, but not *this way*, his heart giving out in shocked response to the Horror's attack.

"You're not responsible for what happened," I told him firmly. "The Horror is."

Reece snatched up his pen.

The Nyktomorph was visiting him. Talking to him for months! I didn't realize it. You don't think that nearly killed Dad?

I couldn't reassure him. He was too close to his father to see it any other way. Gazing levelly at me, he wrote:

Remember all those times he ran away from the house? Going out in his bare feet over all that glass?

"When you thought he was looking for your mum?"

Reece nodded.

He was trying to get away, wasn't he? He knew the monster was coming back. That's why he was so desperate to speak to you when you came over that time.

Reece looked so angry that he could barely make his words legible on the paper.

I wouldn't listen, so he tried to talk to you instead.

I leaned towards the bed. "Reece, I didn't listen either."

A groan came from behind Reece's mouth-mask. He looked so livid that I was sure he was going to rip the tube out of his throat. He scrawled:

You were only with him five minutes!

As I tried to find some words to reassure Reece, his eyes closed. A nurse came over, checked his monitors, and told me that the sedation drugs had taken him back under.

While I waited for him to wake again, I spent the rest of the morning searching frantically for any clues that might lead to Nina. I explored well beyond the hospital this time, but still found nothing. Where was she? She'd been alone with the monsters for several hours now. Were they hurting her? Would they even feed her? Did monsters know to do such things? A terrifying image suddenly leapt into my mind: of Nina pleading for her life while the Horror cheerfully repeated her words back, with the Nyktomorph standing alongside, nodding approval.

I returned to Reece later that morning. Although he was still asleep I stayed by his bed, watching him breathe unevenly through his mask. It was early afternoon before he woke again, and this time, with the drugs wearing off, he was more alert.

Urgently scrawling, he shoved his pad at me.

I think I led them to you. The Nyktomorph hung around until you appeared, then set the Horror on me. They were waiting for you to show up. I'm of secondary importance. You're the real prize.

I shook my head, hating the way he was taking the blame for everything. Holding his shoulders, I said emphatically, "How do you know I didn't lead them to *you*?"

When he started to pick up his pad again, I snatched it from him, writing in heavy, underlined letters:

EVEN iF YOU LED THEM TO ME,

WE WERE DESTINED TO MEET.

WE'RE MEANT TO BE TOGETHER, REECE.

I showed him what I'd written, daring him to deny it. It was a bold thing to write, but I felt it was true, and it came from my heart, and I wanted Reece to know that.

He spent a long time gazing at me, even longer considering his reply. His hand hovered over the page for over a minute. Seeing his fingers twitching, I touched them, felt their warmth. He squeezed me back, then wrote:

We shouldn't be together. Not anymore. My throat's no good to you now. If they got everything inside, I'll be useless. I'm useless anyway. Even the little one, the Horror, was just playing with me in the ward. If

I spread my hand over the page, stopping him from writing.

"It doesn't matter if your throat isn't a weapon anymore," I said. Did I have to spell it out for him? "Reece, I can't do this without you."

That didn't placate him, though. The opposite.

Don't wait until I'm better, Savannah. Get away now. The longer you hang around here protecting me, the easier it is for them to target you. That's what the monsters want. I bet that's why the Horror left me alive—so you'd be here now, distracted by me, instead of looking out for them.

I didn't reply at once. I knew Reece might be right. But I couldn't imagine my life without him now.

"We'll decide what to do when you can talk again," I said.

He shook his head, wrote:

Don't avoid the subject. I might not be able to talk at all when they remove this tube. The doctors are being evasive whenever I ask that question.

"You couldn't talk properly before anyway," I said jokingly, but it came out wrong, sounding as if I'd always found the squeak in his voice ridiculous. I started to apologize, but when I looked back at Reece's face he was smiling. It was the first real smile I'd seen from him since the attack. He knew exactly what I'd meant. I didn't need to explain. Picking up his pad, he wrote:

I'll be the strong, silent type.

As I read it, I could see him laughing until the pain overcame him. Then he edged down the bed, wincing as he tried to find a more comfortable position. I briefly saw one of the claw marks the Horror had made. It cut into the flesh above his right thigh.

"Let me look," I said.

He shook his head, no.

"I just want to see what it did to you."

He shook his head harder—a look of embarrassment. I understood why. I don't know how he'd pictured us together, but it wasn't this way: me like a nurse at his side, him prostrate, covered in disfiguring scars. He obviously hated me seeing him like this.

"You think I feel anything less for you because of what you look like?" I said. "Is that what you believe? That you're not handsome enough for me anymore?"

I coaxed him until he stopped holding the sheets and let me gently part the hospital gown around both sets of scars. It was tricky because he still had clips, catheters, and all sorts of drips draped over and under him. I had to move these out of the way carefully. The most awkward was a tube that went directly into his groin. I didn't try moving this, but it was a delicate act to get his gown past it. I nearly gave up when it was taking too long, but Reece, obviously deciding he might as well finish the job now, finally tugged his gown away far enough so I could see all the damage.

There were four scars. Each was about a foot long, below his waist on either side of his body. Both sets of scars were wide enough to need stitches. I counted nineteen on one side, more on the other.

I carefully ran a finger around the inflamed areas, lightly brushing Reece's skin. I didn't even know why I was doing something so intimate. I just wanted . . . contact with him. To touch him. Reece let me for a few seconds, then turned away, his eyes red with tears.

"What is it?" I murmured.

His hand trembled as he wrote:

Is there anything left in my throat? I've asked the doctors, but they don't know what I'm talking about. I have to know. I've felt my neck on the outside, but I'm all numb from scar tissue.

"It doesn't matter," I said.

That angered him.

It does matter. You of all people know that. The monsters won't stop until they kill you. I'm sure of that now. Stop talking to me like I talked to Dad—ignoring what's important. What matters most to you in this life, Savannah Grey?

I shook my head, not sure how to answer—or even that there was any answer beyond my relationships with Reece and Nina.

He wrote:

The most important thing in my life is you. I knew it the moment we met. But there's no point staying close unless I can defend you with my throat. If I can't, I'll only hold you back. And if I do that I'll be helping them—the Nyktomorph and Horror. I won't do that.

"You've got to concentrate on getting well again," I murmured, playing for time. "I don't want to talk about separating yet."

He wrote:

Accept it. I have.

I lowered my eyes. It was the last thing I wanted him to say.

"We'll think about it after they take the tubes out," I rasped. "We'll decide then. Not before."

Reece gave me a steely look, then turned his face away.

A few hectic hours followed, with hospital nurses changing shift, and everyone around Reece looking more nervous now word had spread that he was at the center of the Horror's attack. But I stayed with him, and not long after that he was transferred out of ICU into a standard ward. I held onto his gurney during the move, and he forced me to accept one thing: that as soon as they took the tube out of his throat, I'd check it. Check it and be honest with him about what was in there.

I agreed to do that. Privately, though, if the news was bad, I knew I wouldn't tell him the whole truth. Not straightaway. I didn't want to jeopardize his recovery. I didn't want to give him the excuse he needed to leave me, either.

In the end they removed all of Reece's tubes in a private room. When I came to see him afterwards the first thing he did was to speak. Well, whisper.

"This is top volume," he announced hoarsely, struggling to enunciate each word.

"You sound great to me," I said, wanting to kiss him.

He sipped tiny quantities of water, giving me a self-deprecating smile. "The Horror didn't get my vocal cords. They say my voice'll probably get back to normal in a few weeks—or normal for me. You know, Mickey Mouse."

"Nothing wrong with Mickey Mouse," I told him, unable to stop grinning. "I happen to like Mickey Mouse."

The mood should have been quietly celebratory, but by the time I sat down and Reece had taken a couple more sips of water he was serious again. "You ready?" he asked. He flashed a tight grin, but now the moment had come to look into his throat I could see how nervous he was.

"We shouldn't do this straightaway," I resisted, wanting to keep the mood light, delay things.

"No. I don't want to wait. It's OK, I know how you feel, but this is hard enough. Let's do it."

He opened his mouth. It was a painful process, taking so much time that other patients in the ward recoiled in alarm. By the time his lips were wide enough, Reece's face was covered in sweat. Only sheer determination seemed to get him through it.

"OK," I murmured. "That's far enough. I can see."

I bent towards Reece. It meant getting close to his lips—the first time I'd put my face near anyone since Olly and the anesthetist looked inside my mouth. And instantly, predictably, from my throat came a set of menacingly slow *clicks*.

With real difficulty, I controlled them, held my mouth shut. The last thing I wanted to do was frighten Reece. Keeping my expression neutral, I smiled at him.

And then I gazed into his mouth. Gazed deeply inside.

And there was . . . nothing.

Nothing at all.

Nothing but those horrifying surgical scars. All the subtle honey-colored and chocolate-brown structures were gone.

"It looks fine," I said.

I knew it would break his heart if I told him, but how could I hide the truth?

He knew. Of course he knew. And gave me a forlorn smile. He looked as if he was trying to say something as well, but the words wouldn't come out.

Instead, clenching his teeth, he found his pad and wrote:

I love you, Savannah Grey.

He wasn't crying, but I was. I leaned close to his poor injured mouth. I stroked his lips with my trembling hands. My throat was buzzing forebodingly, but I thought if I did it fast enough I could make it, just this once sneak a kiss past them. Reece seemed to have the same thought as well, because his eyes misted over and his lips parted naturally.

I dropped my face towards his. I almost reached him. I even grazed his lips, but before I could do anything more one of my own hands thrust itself between us.

Blocking my mouth, it threw me violently across the room.

Reece stared at me aghast as I picked myself off the floor and made my way in tears out of the ward.

24

Initially, the Nyktomorph fulfilled every expectation of the Ocrassa. It loved nothing more than to please its master. And with appropriate training, it matured into a confident, proficient killer. But even the willing Nyktomorph could do nothing to prevent the next attack from nature.

This time the assault came from the sky, but not in any form the Ocrassa had seen before. A secret storm blistered in the north of the world before suddenly heading south and hurling down a forest of trees.

The Ocrassa had not anticipated this. Teeth, yes. Animals, yes. Birds of prey. But the sight of full-sized boughs raining down from the clouds momentarily bewildered it—and that was enough for a single vast cedar to block the path back to its lair.

The Nyktomorph, desperate to do its duty, stood in the way of a smaller tree heading for its master, but its efforts were not enough. Two immense trunks spun from the heart of the storm to flatten the entire rear half of the Ocrassa's body. Leaves then burst from the same trees' branches, thrusting at the Ocrassa's eyes, filling its mouth.

Squirming frenziedly towards its secondary lair, the Ocrassa only made it underground again by hacking off two-thirds of its own trapped limbs.

It was years before the Ocrassa was strong enough to return to the surface, and on that first day back into clear sunlight, it asked the Nyktomorph to accompany it on a walk. The morning sky was an icy blue, and together they examined a lone elm tree near the lair. The Ocrassa exposed the tree's roots, cut them, hacked them in key places. Then it moved on to another tree, and did the same.

"Learn," the Ocrassa said to the Nyktomorph. "Trees are a soil-based organism, and this is how you destroy them. First split the roots. Do that time and again, before they can recover. Then prune and amputate the leaves. But not all of them. You don't want the tree to die too soon. Finally, having kept it alive in this starved state as long as possible, do one last thing."

"Poison it?" the Nyktomorph guessed.

"Burn it."

"Why?"

"Because to burn is the most frightening way for anything to die."

"I see," said the Nyktomorph, eager to participate in its master's revenge.

Thereafter, night after night, trees were cut and tortured and set alight, until there was nowhere for the Nyktomorph to rest without the ash from the fires creasing its nostrils.

Then the Ocrassa moved on to another region and killed those trees as well.

And another.

And another.

Each time it made the Nyktomorph kindle the fires and watch.

"Will we stop now?" the Nyktomorph asked one day.

"No."

The tree deaths went on for years, then decades, until the Nyktomorph became old with watching, but no matter how old it became the Ocrassa had ways of keeping it alive and did so. And finally the day arrived when the Nyktomorph did not so eagerly emerge from its daytime lair to kindle the flames and observe the spectacle of the bonfires.

"Why do you continue to do this?" it asked the Ocrassa one evening, when the flames were especially high. "Has there not been punishment enough?"

Nearby a patch of bamboo was ablaze. The bamboo leaves burned like they had grown: fast. The Nyktomorph stood solemnly, its face blackened with smoke.

"You think to kill this tree is a disgraceful death?" the

Ocrassa asked, furious with its creation. "A dishonoring of something noble?"

And to make sure its defender understood that there could never be too much death associated with its protection, it held the Nyktomorph over the bamboo stalks and seared its face until it could no longer scream.

25

I left my kiss and Reece behind. Shut myself away. Found a windowless room the hospital cleaners used to store equipment, and hid. My feet sloshed through spilled detergent, but I didn't care. I'd let the monsters take Nina, and now I was losing Reece as well. If he left me, I wouldn't even be able to protect him.

I don't know how long I stayed in that cluttered storage space, but the next I knew there was heavy pounding on the door. It was so loud my first thought was to wonder if it was the monsters. Would a monster knock? To disarm me, it might. To make me think it was human. *The Nyktomorph might.*

Then I heard an urgent voice. "Savannah? Are you in there?"

It was Reece, and he sounded terrified. I opened the door to find him standing in the corridor, his face darkened by leaves.

"What are you doing out of bed?" I said automatically. Then I saw orderlies and nurses running behind him, also swiping at leaves. "In here," I said, dragging Reece towards an office. Shutting the door behind us, I made sure he was OK. Then I stared out of the office's main window. The view should have been a panorama of the city's south, but only one thing was visible.

"The leaves are everywhere!" Reece cried. "Don't you know what's been going on? Planes are being diverted and everything. The news is full of it." He shook his head in exasperation at my confusion. "Sav, every tree for miles around is *bare*. Someone saw you go in that room." His voice caught. "I thought something had happened to you. I remembered you saying the leaves were following you. I had to make sure you were OK."

I stroked his face, then felt the wind outside howl. If anything, even more leaves choked the sky here than over Alfredo's café. In great long arcs they flowed back and forth: hectic flurries of aspen, holly, pine, and crack willow.

"What are you doing?" Reece yelled, as I pressed my face against the glass.

"Stand back," I said, holding him at arm's length. "It's me they want."

"You?" Reece blinked in disbelief, but there was no time to wait for him to understand. Outside, clouds were being scattered, birds swept aside.

I knew I couldn't deny the leaves a second time. I had to be out there, part of them.

Stepping forward, I opened the window. Reece tried hauling me back—"Get away from there, Sav!"—but a gust knocked him off his feet.

In the second it took me to pick Reece off the floor, the room became richly, almost impossibly, filled with leaves. They weren't dry autumn castoffs. Each leaf was bright and young. Something had freshly torn them from their branches and brought them to this place to press against me.

A maple leaf suddenly brushed my cheek, giving up its moisture to my lips.

"Reece," I breathed, "they only want me . . . to listen."

Gasping, I ran to the window. In the sky overhead every single leaf was flowing eastwards on the wind. The pattern, I knew now, had been there all the time. For days the leaves had been heading unerringly in that single direction, sinking towards a line of trees. How could I have misunderstood what I was being shown for so long?

I even recognized the place. Dulwich Wood. I'd walked in it many times.

A monster in a wood.

Was my monster there?

It had to be.

I glanced at Reece, and he stood back, looking suddenly afraid. I knew why. A steady grinding cadence of active tics had started belting from my throat. *Ready, you're ready*, they were telling me, and knowing that was true a thread of anticipation surged through my whole body.

Something *was* waiting for me, after all. I'd dreamt about it, but it wasn't a dream; it was real, and now I had to go there to confront it.

The leaves around me abruptly sheared away eastwards, sweeping like the tail of a comet across the sky. "Stay here," I told Reece, gripping his arm. "You can't go where I'm heading." But I wasn't confident of that—wasn't quite sure of myself yet—and perhaps it showed in my eyes because he shook his head firmly.

"I'm staying with you," he insisted. He had to yell to make himself heard over the rustling leaves.

"You don't know what you're up against," I told him.

"Neither do you. Stop arguing with me." He took my hand. "I can't miss this either. You said we were meant to be in this together." I saw his determination to stay with me. And I relented. I nodded.

We ran outside, and leaves instantly surrounded my body—separating me from Reece. I forced a path back to him, but the leaves fought hard to keep me to themselves. They only gave up trying when I held Reece's wrist so they couldn't divide us.

We made our way towards Dulwich Wood on foot. I didn't hurry. Reece was still too ill to rush, but in any case, I sensed that the monster would still be inside when we arrived. And whatever that monster was, I knew it would be even more frightening than the Nyktomorph or the Horror. In my dreams I'd sensed something indescribably sinister. A third monster. More elusive than the others. Something the Nyktomorph and Horror merely served.

Nina, I thought, closing my eyes, *be alive.*

The sun was well below the horizon by the time we reached the outskirts of Dulwich Wood. The trees were almost dark. The black steel gates were padlocked, too, but that didn't hold us up. I simply smashed the chain.

Inside it should have been quiet as late as this, but the trees were alive with chittering. I sensed every bird was awake, and not just the birds. The undergrowth crackled as well with the agitated feet of small mammals. I was swept by a wonderful clarity of purpose. *The whole of nature is showing me the way.*

Reece gazed nervously at the trees. "Sav, do you know what you're doing?"

I shook my head, keeping him close.

"But I don't understand," he said. "What are you expecting to find here?"

A monster, I thought. As I strode with Reece into the thicker trees, birds took flight and led me further inside. A barn owl traversed a stretch of horse chestnuts, calling to other birds, who called back, leading me on.

Reece stumbled on the dark trails, but I held him upright. Looking outward, I licked my lips, and the scent of the earth was suddenly as live to me as the tongue in my mouth. Nature had been waiting for me to be ready for this. For a brief moment I felt myself swept up in its longing. And in that instant, I was the stars of autumn and all the singing birds.

But where was I being led? I had no idea. I could only trust.

We arrived at the southern end of the wood where the trees were broadest. One by one the birds alighted in nearby branches and fell silent, until all I could hear was the clicking of bills and the shaking out of wing feathers.

I'm ready for this, I thought. *I am.*

Vast piles of leaves were underfoot. It was as if every leaf blowing over the past few days had ended up here for me to find. And now that I had made my way to this spot, at last a new breeze rose up. It came out of nowhere, scything low across the ground, molding the leaves into a funnel shape, extending vertically. The funnel was joined by a myriad of birds and even insects, until they formed a coiling vortex over a small clearing.

As soon as I understood that the clearing was my destination, the vortex collapsed, swirling apart. The leaves dropped to the ground, the birds and insects flew back to their nests and homes. They had done all they could to guide me.

"You're going after the monster, aren't you?" Reece whispered.

"I have to. Nina's there."

"Don't," he said, straining to see beyond the trees. "I . . . I didn't think it would be like this."

"You think I should run from it?"

"Yes. You should keep running."

I nearly kissed him when he said that. I wanted to more than anything. He was only trying to protect me.

But this is where it lives, I realized, my heart lurching with a kind of exultant terror. *This is its lair. I can't go back now. Nature has led me to this place.*

Pushing through a tangle of branches, I stepped into the clearing.

Would there be defenses?

Of course.

I saw them almost immediately. Living creatures, waiting for me. Animals of some kind—or approximations of animals. I'd never seen anything like them before.

"They look like pigs," Reece gasped, squinting into the darkness. "No, they look like dogs."

26

Pigs? Dogs? I didn't know what they were, but my eyes fast-flickered, hurriedly trying to calculate the level of danger. There was no sign of Nina, but at least my throat felt prepared, whirring with quiet anticipation. I welcomed that. I'd never felt more certain I needed its protection.

In front of me and Reece were at least forty of the pig-dogs. They stood two rows deep, a solid wall guarding whatever was behind the clearing. There was no obvious pack leader, nothing to mark out one animal from another, but they had definitely spotted us, and I had no doubt they were prepared to defend to the death whatever they were guarding.

"We can't go that way," Reece said, as I strode forward.

He was right. I could approach because I could fight—or run if I had to—but Reece, injured as he was, couldn't do either. I'd agreed to let him come with me, said yes far too easily, and now I knew I'd led him into appalling danger.

It was as I looked for a way to retreat that the Nyktomorph eased into view. Like a deft pocket of nightmare, it dropped in reptilian silence in front of the pig-dogs, moonlight glinting off its facial scars. Moments later, joyful squeals pierced the wood as the Horror joined it. The happiest child could not have been happier as the Horror bounded lightly among the trees. Raking an excited claw through its blond wig, it clearly couldn't wait for the fight to begin.

I glanced between the Nyktomorph—silent and unmoving—and the Horror, which never stopped moving.

They're prepared. They're ready for this. I've led us into a trap.

Beside me, Reece's expression was forlorn.

"Where's Nina?" I demanded, shouting to hide my panic.

The Nyktomorph gestured behind it. The Horror gleefully cooed "Nina, Nina, Nina" and thumped the soil.

Underground, I realized. But why were they showing me that? To lure me down there?

Tonelessly, the Nyktomorph said, "You were rash running in here unprepared like this, Savannah. Why did you bring Reece along? Because you were afraid to face the danger on your own?"

I didn't reply. Not for the first time I grasped how little I knew about the Nyktomorph, while it seemed to know a great deal about me. I studied its body language for some indication of what it might do next, but unlike the Horror, the Nyktomorph never gave away its intentions. It stood absolutely still against the darkness of the trees and the shadowy pig-dogs.

Beckoning at Reece with a claw, the Nyktomorph said, "Come here, to my side."

"No," I said to Reece, my heart racing.

"Do it now," the Nyktomorph ordered Reece, "or the Horror will kill Nina, and I will kill Savannah myself."

Reece stared at the two monsters as if he couldn't decide which was the worst. Then, glancing hopelessly at me, he started walking towards them.

"Don't," I said, desperately trying to come up with a plan to get us out of this. My throat was ticking, beginning to warm up, but only slowly. Could it stop both the Nyktomorph and the Horror before one of them murdered Reece? Perhaps. But the pig-dogs, staying rigidly in their lines guarding the clearing, were an unknown factor. And how could I even begin to fight without knowing where Nina was?

I looked around, agonizingly aware that if I made even a single mistake now both the people I cared most about might be dead in the next few moments. Especially if the Horror got its way. It was obviously frustrated, eager to hurt something. Traces of liquid shone on its quivering prongs, beading the upper ends.

"Too slow," said the Nyktomorph. "I will not ask again. Reece, come this way."

"No, don't move," I insisted.

"The Nyktomorph says it'll kill you," Reece said.

"If you go the Nyktomorph will have you *and* Nina. That's what they want."

"But can you fight them?" Reece whispered. "Can you?" When he saw from my face that I had no idea, he shut his eyes and took another step forward. Blood seeped through the torn fabric of his jeans. The left-side stitches had reopened.

I trembled, checking the trees. If this was a trap the third monster must be here as well. The real monster. Where was it? Hiding underground? Possibly. More likely watching me from some concealed location, learning about me while I learned nothing about it. But whatever the risk, I couldn't just let Reece walk into the Nyktomorph's claws.

"If you leave now," the Nyktomorph said to me, "I will make sure that Reece and Nina are not hurt."

That was unexpected. Was it mocking me? Whatever the truth, I had no reason to believe it.

"What are you waiting for?" Reece hissed. "Sav, get out of here! It's letting you go! Run!"

He tottered forward. You could see that the last thing Reece wanted to do was approach anything as large as the Nyktomorph, but he did so because—deadly though the Nyktomorph was—nobody could have made themselves walk towards the Horror.

I let Reece get a short distance from me. I had to. My only chance was to play for time until my throat offered me other options. I felt much more in control of it now. It was ready to act, hostile clicks building, but I didn't have a clear target yet—not without endangering Nina and Reece.

How could I get the monsters to show me where Nina was? There had to be a way.

"Take me in exchange for them both," I called out.

The Nyktomorph considered this.

"No," it said—and in a single leap, much faster than I expected, lunged for Reece. Grasping him with one claw, it held him by the throat.

Reece stiffened and spluttered, his feet kicking and jerking in midair.

"You . . . you don't need to do that!" I yelled, my mind blazing with fear. "He's hurt. He—"

"Then leave! Go now!" the Nyktomorph roared—the first time it had raised its voice.

"Nina, where are you?" I shouted.

Silence. I tried to think of another way to bargain, but couldn't find one.

And then we all heard a voice. It came from underneath us. A girl's voice. Singing. Or trying to. A carol. "Silent Night." Sung hesitantly and very slowly and with almost no energy.

"*Silent night, holy night,*
All is calm, all is bright . . ."

I knew in that moment that Nina was trying to let me know where she was without risking the wrath of the Horror, and, thinking about how much she must have suffered before she learned this way of appeasing it, a great throb of pity ran through me. But at the same time, it was an opportunity. If she could distract the Horror—and I could concentrate solely on the Nyktomorph—we might have a chance.

I heard a choked-back "help me" from Nina somewhere low to my left, followed by a muffled sob, but the Nyktomorph blocked my path that way.

"Keep singing," I told her. "I need the Horror to lead me to you."

I didn't know if Nina understood what I was trying to do, but she carried on her fitful tune. The Nyktomorph quickly saw how agitated the Horror was becoming, but couldn't stop it scampering to the edge of the clearing. Hooting at the ground—a shrill imitation of Nina—the Horror thrust its arms into a concealed hole and hauled her neck-first out of the ground.

My heart flew into my mouth as I saw Nina's mud-spattered white shirt. Was she injured? Covered in dirt, it was impossible to tell. Her expression was flat as well, dulled by sheer weariness. But somehow she continued weakly holding the tune of the carol.

I glanced around. There was still no sign of the third monster, but at last I could see everyone who mattered to me. Time to act.

I shouted at Nina to stop singing, and as she did—with the Horror bending down to slap her, make her continue—my throat erupted. A spread of hard *clicks* shot out, flowing from the middle of my lips. The Horror was closest, but I turned my mouth towards the more dangerous Nyktomorph. The shimmering cluster of noises that flashed out caught it by surprise, cutting into its flank.

Startled, it dropped Reece.

"Run!" I shouted at him. "Any direction!"

Reece hesitated, then did so, crashing through the trees.

I spun around to face the Horror, but with unbelievable speed it had already snatched Nina and dragged them both back inside the hole. At a glance from the Nyktomorph, the pig-dogs surrounded the hole's entrance to prevent me following. But at least Reece was no longer in sight. *Keep running*, I thought, knowing that every moment I kept the Horror and the Nyktomorph here offered him precious seconds to escape.

The Nyktomorph stood erect. My attack had cut into its torso, but the injury was minor and it ignored it. And then it showed me a motion I would have thought beyond anything so huge. With a subtle, sliding movement it jumped across the clearing and somehow squeezed its immense bulk into the hole beside the Horror and Nina.

A single piercing scream from Nina stopped me from attacking it there, and moments later the Horror appeared again at the hole's rim. It lifted Nina over its head, its knee bent under her arched back. I understood: if I didn't leave, it would break her spine.

Then, laughing, it threw Nina high into the air.

As I screamed out, knowing I couldn't reach her in time, the Horror took advantage of my distraction to scramble out from the hole. With a sharp cry, leaving Nina still hanging in the air, it bolted into the trees after Reece. Within half a second it was beyond the range of my throat, scrambling through the branches.

Back at the hole, the Nyktomorph safely caught the falling Nina. Shocked and relieved at the same time, I tried to work out where the Horror had gone. Reece was nowhere in sight, but I knew it wouldn't take the Horror long to track him down.

Watching me, still unhurried—always supremely un-hurried—the Nyktomorph softly cradled Nina's neck.

I had to go after the Horror. What choice did I have? In this mood, so provoked and excited, it was bound to kill Reece. But that meant abandoning Nina. I couldn't do that.

I had to choose between them, but how could I?

The Nyktomorph's expression was unreadable. Nina's head sat like a tiny pebble in its claws. Then a shriek of pure eagerness from the Horror pierced the woods be-hind me. I gazed desolately at the Nyktomorph. I'd never imagined looking for help from a monster before, but now, with all my heart, I prayed that I was right and that the Nyktomorph had more control over its instincts than the Horror.

With one final agonized glance at Nina, I ran after Reece.

27

Despite the burning of much of the world's forests, the trees gradually returned.

The Nyktomorph's devotion to its master, however, was never the same. It began to bed down with the pig-dogs, preferring their company. And one day it went further: freeing an animal involved in one of the Ocrassa's pain-filled hybrid experiments. As punishment, the Ocrassa tied the Nyktomorph to a rock and cut its face in several places. Inside those cuts it inserted mounds of soil. Soon fast-growing plants like ivy coiled and thrived there. The Nyktomorph's smile became a twisted maple that had taken root in its lip.

Eventually the Ocrassa released the Nyktomorph again, expecting a return to compliance. But instead the Nyktomorph became even more taciturn. It began to question everything: its purpose, the nature of suffering, why it was killing at all. It endlessly queried the simplest of instructions.

Then, subtly, the Nyktomorph learned ways to actually disobey. Not directly—its brain-design and early obedience training were too thorough to permit outright rebellion— but in small, understated, ways. Impossible though it was for the Nyktomorph to violate the Ocrassa's commands altogether, it managed to perform all the tasks set it inefficiently.

It even tried to kill itself by throwing its body from a mountaintop. The Ocrassa watched nervously as the suicide attempt failed, relieved that at least that part of the Nyktomorph's early conditioning was still intact.

Failing suicide, though, the Nyktomorph spent decades seeking to break its obedience conditioning. It could not quite do this, but it never gave up trying.

"I will kill you now," said the Ocrassa one day.

"Yes," came the relieved answer.

The Ocrassa was inclined to. Why not? The Nyktomorph was just another experiment that had gone wrong. But so much effort had been invested in this one. There might not be time to construct another defender before the next battle with nature. Then the Ocrassa had another idea. It had seen the way family ties increased bonding in the pig-dogs. Perhaps all the Nyktomorph needed was an offspring. Would giving it a child bring it around to obedience again? Curious, the Ocrassa studied this problem objectively.

"What do you want your baby to look like?" it asked one day. "Like you? If it looks like you, will that increase your affection for it?"

"No," the Nyktomorph replied.

"Do you have no opinion on the appearance of your child?" the Ocrassa asked, unperturbed.

This time there was no response from the Nyktomorph. Then it murmured, "Do not make it...intelligent."

"Why?"

The Nyktomorph refused to answer.

"Will you obey me if I do not create an intelligent creature? If I create something dumb?"

A brief hesitation, then: "No."

"I need you to obey me."

"No."

"What will make you obey me again?"

"Nothing willingly."

"Then I will make something you despise."

The Ocrassa set to work. Deciding on a new design, it fashioned the Horror. It did not name it the Horror. The Nyktomorph did that, seeing what it grew into. The Ocrassa adapted one of the pig-dog's brains for its new creation, but gave it a flexible, feisty, canine body combined with suckers as well as claws.

"If you continue to resist me, I will make an abomination," the Ocrassa said. "It will be like one of my hybrid experiments. You don't like those, do you?"

"Nothing you do or say will change my behavior now."

"We will see."

The Ocrassa fashioned a star-shaped head for the Horror. It was deliberately clumsy. The edges of the prongs caught on things. "If I make the head more rounded," the Ocrassa said to the Nyktomorph, "will you obey me?"

"No."

So the Ocrassa went further. After completing the awkward head, it created a superfluous gland in the Horror's neck. Liquid spurted from this gland, pouring continuously from the Horror's mouth. This did not radically impair the Horror's efficiency, but it did disturb the Nyktomorph.

"Do not do this," the Nyktomorph said.

"Will you willingly obey me again if I remove the liquid gland?"

"No."

"Then I will go further."

The Ocrassa grafted useless tiny arms in the middle of the Horror's chest.

"Will you obey me now?" it asked.

No answer.

"Will you obey me if I remove the arms and the throat gland and improve the shape of the head?"

No answer.

The Ocrassa, satisfied that it had finally shocked the Nyktomorph into silence, continued to work on the Horror. Copying nature, it grew pliable skin. "I will make your baby soft, so it is enjoyable to hold," it said.

The Nyktomorph glanced up slowly. "Any child you make is yours, not mine."

"Eyes?" the Ocrassa asked.

"Make it blind," the Nyktomorph whispered.

"Why?"

"So it does not have to see you."

Amused, the Ocrassa crafted for the Horror a single, delicate, cobalt-blue eye.

The Nyktomorph murmured, "I will break this conditioning. I will break it and find a means to kill you. One way or another, I will do so."

"I want you to look after this child," the Ocrassa said confidently. "All true parents care for their children."

"Parents?" The Nyktomorph tried to hide its nervousness. "I am no parent."

"I have seen the way certain animals bear their own offspring from a womb," the Ocrassa said. "Such a birth method bonds them, parent to child. For the last part of the Horror's development I will do the same for you. You will give birth. You will bear the Horror inside your own body."

Tying the Nyktomorph down, the Ocrassa grafted a womb into its belly. "This will increase the connection between you and it," the Ocrassa said. "Do you want a male or female offspring?"

No answer. The Nyktomorph had stopped speaking altogether.

The gestation period was a long one. For two whole years the blood tissues of the Horror and the Nyktomorph were joined. For the second of those years the Nyktomorph felt the Horror's heart beating inside it, the long legs kicking.

In the last stages, the Ocrassa inserted milk ducts onto the Nyktomorph's torso.

And at last there was a birth.

The Horror uncurled and lifted its star-head inquisitively. Its prongs opened and its childish legs quivered.

But the Nyktomorph refused to look at what had been born.

"Care for it," the Ocrassa said.

"No."

"You must feed it."

"No."

"You refuse?"

"Yes."

"Then it will die, and it will be your fault, not mine."

"Please," the Nyktomorph begged, knowing that begging would make no difference. "Do not do this. It is alive now. You made it. You must look after it."

"Will you obey me if I do?"

"No."

"Then it will starve."

The Horror was left alone on the ground. For several days it wailed with hunger in the dirt, its blue eye imploring both the Nyktomorph and the Ocrassa to nourish it.

The Nyktomorph did not once look at the Horror after it was born. It knew that it would only grow up to be a killer like the Ocrassa. Days passed, during which the Ocrassa secretly provided the Horror sustenance—just enough food to keep it alive and crying out with its baby-lungs.

A month went by this way.

One morning, with the Horror's plaintive cries ringing in the air as always, the Nyktomorph gave the Ocrassa a stare that was pure venom.

"Yes," said the Ocrassa. "That is what I bred you for. Give that fierceness back to me."

"Never."

"I have been feeding the Horror," the Ocrassa said. "All this time, I have kept it alive. It is quite large now. You should look at it."

"I will not."

"You should at least nourish it, for I will no longer do so."

The Ocrassa stopped feeding the Horror. It became weaker and weaker, and quieter. One night, when it was almost dead with starvation, a freezing wind swept in from the north. The wind stippled the Horror's pale naked skin with frost, making it mewl piteously. And just once— knowing this was nearly the end—the Nyktomorph raised its head. Determined to honor the dying child with at least one moment of recognition, it glanced the Horror's way.

And in that one look the Nyktomorph was lost. It had not known what would happen to its heart. For now that it had looked upon the Horror's famished face, it could not abandon it. Instead, unable to stop its legs, it walked across to the Horror and held its star-points. At the same time, it turned to the Ocrassa, which was watching in delight nearby.

"Nature must even now be creating a weapon that will kill you," the Nyktomorph said.

The Ocrassa admitted that—the Nyktomorph throwing its greatest fear at it.

It allowed time to pass, for the bond to develop between the Nyktomorph and the Horror. Soon they began going off together on long walks and dolefully staring at their reflections in bodies of water. Then, when it felt the bond was sufficiently established, the Ocrassa said to the Nyktomorph, "You will obey me now. You will do so or I will kill your child."

"I knew you would say that," the Nyktomorph replied. "I have prepared the Horror for death as best I can, and I wish to die. Surely you understand that?"

The Ocrassa did not understand. Nothing in its own genes enabled it to understand.

"Obey me," it demanded.

"No."

"Then accept the consequences."

The Ocrassa took the Horror and impassively beat it (without injuring the eye, which was difficult to repair). The Nyktomorph, witnessing the violence, gazed furiously at the Ocrassa.

"Good," the Ocrassa said, glad to see the flame back in the Nyktomorph's stare. "Nurture the child. Teach it to protect me."

"I will teach it nothing for which you do not give me specific orders."

"Then I will teach it myself. I will make it more dependable, and replace you with it, and then I will kill you."

"What will you teach it?"

"To love me."

The Nyktomorph laughed loudly. "Nothing can love you."

The Ocrassa was shocked by the certainty with which the Nyktomorph said this.

"How do you know nothing can love me?"

The Nyktomorph merely lidded its eyes and gazed back in silence.

It does not want me to understand, the Ocrassa sensed. Therefore, I must.

Ripping the Horror away from the Nyktomorph, the Ocrassa kept the Horror close and cared for it. Imitating what it had seen in mammal behavior, it nuzzled it, whispered to it, kept it warm at night.

And some things worked out the way the Ocrassa intended. The Horror grew up, with training, into an adequate enough killer. But it never loved the Ocrassa. And when the Horror needed comfort it was invariably to the Nyktomorph that it went. The Horror never forgot the early beating, either. And once it discovered that the Ocrassa had created its star-head, vestigial arms, and throat-gland out of spite, it learned disobedience in its own way, becoming impatient and unpredictable, staying forever in a childlike state, not capable of anything else, a wild spirit.

And then, one day, increasingly frustrated, the Ocrassa stumbled across its first human—and everything changed.

28

I crashed through Dulwich Wood, but there was no trace of Reece. No yellow drips to track him with either in the darkness. I was just beginning to lose all hope, and think of heading back to Nina, when he finally answered his mobile—"Savannah?"

I almost collapsed with relief at the sound of his voice. Then I noticed how strained it was, barely above a whisper. "Your throat's hurt again, isn't it?" I said, my heart pounding.

Reece's answer was interrupted by a noise. It sounded like a man shouting at his end of the line. A female shriek came straight after it, cleaving the air.

I knew only one creature that could make someone shriek like that.

"Reece," I said, already plotting a course out of the wood as I ran. "Quickly, tell me where you are."

"I've nearly made it back to the hospital," he muttered hoarsely. "Sav, I . . . I don't feel so good."

Over the phone connection, there came a faint *pas pas*.

"Get inside. Anywhere," I told him, trying to contain my emotions. "I can reach you in about five minutes, but you've got to get out of sight. Any building will do. Just get off the street so you can't be seen."

I heard the slap of trainers as Reece, obviously ill, tried clumsily to run.

Then an object crashed somewhere behind him. It sounded like a car being upended. A joy-filled bark floated down the line after it, followed by sniffing.

"Did you hear that?" he whispered.

"I heard."

"It's the Horror, isn't it?"

"Yes." There was no point pretending otherwise. I jumped over a van, cutting up a side street. "Reece, you've got to hold on until I can get there. But if the Horror finds you first, co-operate. Whatever happens, don't do anything to excite it."

More uneven slapping of feet. Reece seemed to be falling over every fourth or fifth step. And following his lumbering footfalls came fresher, lighter ones—brisk scampers, interspersed with merry little squeals. For a second, while I sped across the grounds of Alleyn's School, the signal faded. Then I faintly heard Reece cough, followed by a door slamming.

"I'm in one of the hospital blocks," he said shakily. "But I think the Horror's somewhere in here with me."

"Which block?"

"No idea, but I'm in some kind of . . . I think it's an exam room." He coughed again. "The Horror's searching all the rooms in my corridor. It's going to find me, isn't it?"

Another door banged, terrifyingly close to Reece. I heard the sharp crack of a lock being broken.

"Quick, you might still have time to hide somewhere inside your room," I told him.

"You're kidding, aren't you?"

"Isn't there a bed?"

"Yeah, but it's just a platform with a sheet. I can't hide under that!" His voice was panicky now, barely under control. I had to keep him thinking.

"Get under the sheet. Cover yourself."

"That won't work!"

"It might, if you stay still enough."

There was a huge crash in the background, and my chest swelled. I wasn't going to reach Reece in time, and that this might be my last chance to say anything to him, or ever hear his voice again. "Reece . . ." But I choked back what I wanted to say. I didn't dare risk giving away his position to the Horror. It was too close. Instead, to mask the sound of traffic and other noises from my end of the line, I covered my mouthpiece.

For over a minute after that all I heard was Reece's shallow, labored breathing. Then another huge bang— something heavy springing across his room.

Please, I thought.

I had about a kilometer to go. Never taking the phone from my ear, I sprinted through a small hedge and over two main roads. At Reece's end of the line, there was silence. All I heard was static. Was he holding his breath, or had he stopped breathing? The silence extended into a second minute, and I was just about to speak when I finally heard a desperate, ragged intake of air and the clatter of the Horror scampering away.

"Reece?" No answer. For a few unbearable seconds there was only the pounding of blood in my ears. Then he came back on the line. "It's gone," he murmured. "It's—" But I couldn't make out what he said next.

"Reece, I can't hear you."

"I'm so tired." The smallest of voices. "What's the matter with me? I can hardly move my legs."

"You're weak, that's all. You're injured. You just went through an operation, remember? I'm almost there. Stay where you are."

Crossing heavy traffic, I surged like a blur of speed over the brow of Denmark Hill just north of the hospital. Then, as I raced the last downward stretch, I heard more scurrying at Reece's end of the line.

"The Horror's coming back," he whispered.

"Stay in the room if you can," I told him. "It's searched that place, so it probably won't go there again. Don't go into the corridor, where it can see you. Reece, are you listening?"

He wasn't. I heard street sounds as he crashed through an exit.

216

"I'm outside," he yelled, his voice sounding briefly triumphant. A second later, though, his voice faded badly again. "I can't . . . can't . . . "

He coughed, and this time didn't stop for several seconds.

No, I thought. *Hold on. Hold on.*

I was within sight of the hospital now. Reece muttered something about the Hambledon Wing, but the rest of what he said was too slurred to understand.

"Find something to hide behind," I told him. "Just crouch down somewhere."

There was no reply this time, but I was nearly there. Wasting no time, I ran alongside the hospital's high southern fence, vaulted it and headed for the Hambledon Wing. All around me there was chaos. People who'd seen the Horror were spilling in every direction. Patients were being wheeled out by frightened relatives, staff scattering. Someone hit an emergency alarm, and sirens pealed out in great rising waves from the Guthrie Wing.

I was hurtling past the brightly lit main entrance when I saw the Horror burst out of a side door. Its momentum carried it several meters through the air and, as it landed, its suckered feet pivoted, its star-head searching for Reece. It hadn't spotted me yet. Two doctors left the children's ward next door, and for a moment the Horror was distracted, running after their flapping white coats and imitating their screams.

I found Reece crouched behind a thin tree, hopelessly exposed. I ran across and gripped his shoulders. I lifted him up. His face was horribly drained—the color not just of someone tired, but deeply, deeply ill.

"Reece, show me what's wrong?" I knelt down, shielding him with my back.

He bent over, coughing twice. Then he spat something red out.

Our eyes met.

"My throat scars," he rasped. "They're opening. I can't . . . can't breathe." He clutched at me, suddenly fighting for air.

I held him tightly. "I'll find someone. Hold on."

Lifting Reece, I carried him to the emergency room. When I reached it, the front desk was empty. All the doctors and nurses had fled. I kicked open the sliding doors to the ER corridor. Beyond it, there were only silent waiting rooms.

"Help me!" I bellowed. "Someone please help me!"

No answer. Outside, a truncated shriek—the Horror was close.

I lay Reece's body down as softly as I could on the hard orange tiles of the ER corridor. He was shaking uncontrollably now, his eyes unfocused. I shouted for help again, but my calls went unanswered. Trembling, I placed a finger hesitantly inside Reece's mouth to find the injury. It came out soaked in blood.

"Reece, can you hear me?"

He didn't answer. He just lay there. He no longer even seemed aware of me.

No, I won't lose you, I thought, silently screaming. *There has to be someone who can help. I won't let you die like this. I won't.*

I was checking the fastest way to the surgical wing when a blue-uniformed nurse rushed past. "I need your help," I said, seizing her arm. When she tried to push me aside, I held her firmly. "I said I need your help!"

"Get off me!" She gazed anxiously over her shoulder.

I followed her eyes down the corridor. "I know what you're scared of," I said. "I know what's after you." When she still looked distracted, I punched the floor, splintering several tiles. "Look at me!" I yelled. "I'm the only thing that can stop the monster you've seen. I'll protect you from it. I will. All you have to do is help me keep this boy alive."

"He's . . . bleeding heavily," the nurse said, blinking at my arm.

"I can see that! It must be possible to do something."

The nurse shook her head. "Emergency surgery might save his life. But finding someone now . . ." She wriggled to get away from my grasp, clearly frightened of me.

I let go of her arm. Threatening her wasn't going to make her help me. Somehow I had to convince her.

"Please," I said. "I *can* protect you, and I will. Just get Reece some help, and I'll save you and everyone else who can reach this place. Bring them all here. Bring the doctors."

Did she believe me? I couldn't be sure. "Wait," I said, as she headed away. "How do I keep him alive while you're gone?"

"If he has no pulse and he's stopped breathing, do CPR," she said. Without another word she ran from the building.

After she left, all I could hear were distant sounds. Screaming came from somewhere to my left, and what sounded like objects—maybe people—being thrown around. Every minute or so, I took Reece's pulse. It was unsteady, and blood continued to spill out of him. I sat him up, tilted his face on its side, so the blood came out of his mouth instead of going down his throat. Where was the nurse? I waited for her. A minute passed. Two. I felt Reece's pulse again. There was still a faint beat, but he was unconscious. Letting out a groan, I murmured something softly to him. I'm not sure what it was.

A great pool of blood began to spread in a circle around the two of us. I held Reece in my arms, and though every time I bent towards his face my throat was burning to attack him, I quelled it.

Another minute passed, and outside there were more screams.

I felt Reece's pulse again. It was gone. No pulse. His face was ashen. I placed my hand against his mouth to check he was still breathing. I felt nothing. An image suddenly came into my mind of Reece's dad. He'd probably looked down on the one-year-old baby Reece in the garden in the same helpless way I was doing now.

But I'm not helpless, am I? I thought. The nurse told me what to do.

Gritting my teeth, I jerked his shirt completely away from his chest. Then I found the place at his stomach where his ribs met. A fine line of light-brown hair ran from his navel down into his jeans.

I searched for the base of Reece's ribcage. Tightening my fingers, I formed a fist—and shoved. The corridor was so quiet that I could hear the scrunch my knuckles made as they pushed upward. I thrust five times, not sure I was doing it right.

And then I placed my face across his.

My face across his.

How could I do that?

As if to confirm it was a forlorn hope, a thickening array of clicks was building in my throat. Shuddering with the effort, forcing my neck down, I subdued them, fought them back.

Gradually I lowered my face until it hovered over Reece's. But it was almost impossible to keep my mouth so close. Even with him lying underneath me, dying, I could barely make myself do it. And what made it harder was that his mouth was slack and open. I had to part my own lips terrifyingly wide to fit over his. His tongue was dark red. I could smell all the blood inside him. I couldn't do this, but I had to. Pulling back a few centimeters, I took a long drag of air.

And then, fighting my throat the whole way, I reached down to form a seal with Reece's blood-drenched lips.

29

Homo sapiens. A new upright bipedal species.

As soon as the Ocrassa invaded the nervous system of its first human being, it understood that it had found something remarkable. Feverish with excitement, it headed north up the body until it came to the cranium. It was then, and only then, that the Ocrassa realized it had discovered not just something new but what it had sought and waited for its entire life—the *ne plus ultra*, the ultimate point of evolution on this world.

Eons ago, the Ocrassa had reached a position where it could easily destroy every living creature on Earth. In moments of fear, it had often wanted to do just that. But something apart from the prospect of hunger had always restrained it. For millions of years, it had held back in particular from killing the mammals, not quite sure why. Only now did it comprehend the reason for such staggering patience.

It had been waiting for nature to create this pinnacle life-form.

Homo sapiens.

What a remarkable brain it had. Unlike any species on Earth that had come before, given sufficient time that brain could achieve almost anything.

It could, for instance, master the raw secrets of genetics.

That was what the Ocrassa needed it for. Unlike other creatures, the Ocrassa could not reproduce itself biologically. It could not have offspring. But once it developed the technology of genetic engineering, it could manufacture copies of its own genes. That way, it could reproduce itself endlessly, sending wave after wave of its own DNA in seed-pods—billions of them—across the universe.

Indeed, unwittingly, the Ocrassa's own behavior had always been designed to encourage nature to develop a species intelligent enough to battle it. And it was precisely this species—nature's potential weapon—that the Ocrassa used to finish its reproductive cycle.

Armed with this great new insight—and eager to complete itself—the Ocrassa set to work.

It entered the form of the man it had stumbled upon. Careful not to injure him, it delved into his brain, adding its own wide knowledge of biology. But a single human brain, even combined with its own, was not enough to unlock the complex cellular secrets of DNA. The Ocrassa needed the finest brains of countless humans over many generations to achieve that.

So, for the first and only time in its existence, the Ocrassa became a force of creative accomplishment in the world. Using the form of the man, it founded basic science and spread a love of learning. To drive biological advances forward in particular, it became a person of influence and power in the world, changing its human identity from time to time.

So obsessed was the Ocrassa by the task that it almost forgot about the Nyktomorph and the Horror. But it did not quite forget them. It kept them alive and hidden. The Nyktomorph retreated into wary silence. The Horror remained the Horror—a child, perpetually young in its mind. And alongside them the Ocrassa kept breeding the pig-dogs. They might still be useful.

But it also finished developing one other special creature: an ape-hybrid. A primate, but stronger than any ape. Something secret. Something even the Nyktomorph knew nothing of. A body into which the Ocrassa could slip as a last resort.

The human brain amazed the Ocrassa. Such marvelous complexity! And from that brain the Ocrassa finally began to learn about the emotion that had always eluded it.

Love.

The Ocrassa understood now why the Nyktomorph had tried to keep that knowledge to itself. Love was a mysterious, potent force. When moved by love, humans could be influenced to do virtually anything: take insane risks, deny themselves, jeopardize their own safety.

The genetics—the science—was always the Ocrassa's first priority. But while it maintained progress on that, it diverted itself by studying human love in all its forms. For a while it infiltrated the body of a woman, and used her to experience giving birth. The Ocrassa did not love the child it bore, but it felt . . . a vague attachment. A kinship.

Realizing that something fundamental was still missing from its understanding of love, however, the Ocrassa looked at what attracted human males and females. It discovered what scents they liked, what visuals. It crafted irresistible timbres of voice. Found how to whisper persuasively in an ear.

Simultaneously—sure now that nature's attack would come from *Homo sapiens*—the Ocrassa made an intimate study of human anatomy. Finding nothing to concern it in the bodies of the human population in general, it concluded that nature would endow a single individual with an exceptional set of gifts.

That was logical. Harder for the Ocrassa to find one person among many. Harder to prepare for an unknown risk as well.

A single assassin, then.

Nature would send against it a lone sword—an avatar.

The Ocrassa began a search for this human. Better to be the hunter than later become the hunted.

It searched methodically. It was patient. And one day it sensed something. It found a place where nature did not seem to threaten it at all—as if nature did not want it to look there.

The Ocrassa followed its instinct to a city, a set of streets.

There it waited.

And saw her at last.

A girl.

Savannah Grey.

The Ocrassa furtively stalked her for months, relieved to find that as yet she was unaware of her special gifts. Once it knew that, it was tempting to kill her at once—a shock attack of overwhelming force. But the Ocrassa had survived all its life by being cautious, and it did not want to take unnecessary risks now.

How about an attack on her from a distance using artificial means? It might work. But perhaps she had defenses against such things as well. The point was that the first attack on her had to be successful. If it was not, she would know it existed, and killing her would become infinitely harder.

So, with exquisite patience, the Ocrassa covertly watched Savannah Grey.

It discovered that her hands often went to her throat. What was inside there? Too wise to approach her directly, the Ocrassa ordered the Nyktomorph to find out what it could. But the Nyktomorph came to no conclusions—or none it would reveal to the Ocrassa without endless questioning. So instead the Ocrassa sent out the Horror to spy on her. If the Horror was killed or injured in the process, that was no great loss—indeed, if Savannah killed the Horror, it would say much about her fighting capacity.

The Horror perched for days outside Savannah's window and inside her house, hearing strange sounds. It repeated

...se sounds back to the Ocrassa. Frightening sounds. So.

...e had a sonic weapon, throat-based. The Ocrassa had
...me across a fledgling example of this in the dolphins
...at attacked it ages before, but this version seemed sub-
...ntially more refined and formidable.

...Disturbed, the Ocrassa set about developing its own
...uivalent. It pooled all its knowledge from whales, bats,
...d dolphins about the use of sound, but Savannah had
...ignificant head start, and the Ocrassa realized it could
...t catch up in time. Its best chance was to strike quickly,
...w, before her throat-weapon matured.

...But how? No doubt her defenses would be considerable.
...erefore the attack must come from close range.

...How close exactly?

...Close enough to strike directly at her heart and lungs.

...But how to get that close without risking itself?

...Delving into the essence of the human mind, the Ocrassa
...ight an advantage—and found one.

...Love.

...t would convince Savannah Grey to love it.

...t would seduce her.

...Not even a full seduction was needed.

...A kiss would suffice.

...A kiss would fully open up her throat.

...A kiss was perfect.

...t would come close enough to Savannah Grey to obtain a
...gering kiss. From there, it was a straight and short distance
...destroy her throat and her other vital internal organs.

She would not be able to defend herself until it was too late.

Satisfied with its strategy, the Ocrassa began to set up what it needed.

First, a secure location—somewhere close to Savannah's house, but discreet. In the end the Ocrassa chose Dulwich Wood simply because there was no other local area large enough to conceal its lair. Nature's marauding leaves eventually found it there, tried to choke the entrance, but it had defeated them before, and they were no match for the latest version of the Ocrassa.

Then it readied the lair. In an emergency, if all else failed, this place would be its killing ground for Savannah Grey.

Following that, the Ocrassa fetched the Horror and Nyktomorph from the place it had tethered them. In a serious fight, the Horror would be next to useless, but the Nyktomorph was another matter—nothing, truly, could guard it better than a willing Nyktomorph. So the Ocrassa spent months reforging old obedience conditioning. It also gave the Nyktomorph a specific instruction—one it could not ignore or countermand. "You will protect me with your life. When I ask it, you will do everything in your power to kill Savannah Grey."

The only question remaining after that was how the Ocrassa should present itself to Savannah to receive its kiss.

After pondering this, the Ocrassa picked the most natural disguise.

A boy.

The search took a considerable time. Only a creature as patient and knowledgeable as the Ocrassa could have picked exactly the right boy for Savannah. But eventually it found him.

Reece Gandolfo.

His gestures, the way he spoke, his analytical bent of mind, his intelligence, even his sense of humor, all met Savannah's needs more entirely than any boy she would ever have met randomly in her life.

He really was the perfect match for her.

A handsome boy as well, but not overly so—nothing to raise suspicions.

Once it had picked him, the Ocrassa invaded his body and mind. It was far from easy. Reece was mentally strong. He resisted. He fought being taken over more than almost anyone else the Ocrassa had inhabited before. That gave the Ocrassa control problems—Reece's real personality kept bursting through in Savannah's presence—but once those incidents were handled, it only made the Ocrassa more certain that in Reece it had chosen correctly for the even more remarkable Savannah Grey.

But a boy on his own was a vacuum, suspicious.

The Ocrassa needed a family.

Reece's own would do. It was a big one: a mother, father, two girls aged nine and eight, two boys aged seven and five.

By threatening the children, the Ocrassa found it easy to convince the mother and father to pose for extra family photos solely with Reece. It didn't want the complication of the other children in the snapshots. Much easier for Savannah to sympathize with an only child like herself. After the photo shoot, the Ocrassa kept the father, but killed the mother. She was superfluous. It did, however, make use of the family house, located conveniently near Savannah's.

Mr. Gandolfo proved useful. It was only necessary to put his remaining children in danger to get him to cooperate. He redecorated Reece's room. He even shakily framed the new "family photos" neatly on the bedroom wall. After that, the Ocrassa disabled him. Gave him a series of small, precise strokes of the brain. Not violent enough to kill, of course, just sufficient to incapacitate him—and engender sympathy in an outsider.

Even then, Mr. Gandolfo did everything asked of him. It was love that moved him. Knowing his other children were imprisoned in the Ocrassa's lair, as long as the Ocrassa held out hope for them (and for Reece himself), he stayed cooperative even when he sensed that he was slowly dying. However, there was still a slight danger he would speak out, try to warn Savannah. To be on the safe side, the Ocrassa increased the severity of the strokes, so that by the time Savannah visited the house he was almost completely incapacitated.

But not quite. The Ocrassa still gave Mr. Gandolfo a part to play. A story to stutter out. Monsters. I've been visited by a monster! I've seen one! Of course the only monster the father had seen was the Ocrassa itself. But Savannah Grey would not know that.

Mr. Gandolfo served his role well. The Ocrassa became his ever-dutiful son, he the ill but devoted father. A dark secret was even fabricated. Some terrible past guilt that gnawed away at Reece's dad. He just couldn't get over what he'd done to his son's neck. Such a terrible thing to happen. The Ocrassa injured Reece to make the neck wound look real, and worked hard on the details of its story, knowing that no one would appreciate it better than the throat-conscious Savannah.

But getting that first moment of contact right with Savannah Grey was still critical. The Ocrassa had agonized over the best way to do it. If the situation was mishandled, she might become wary.

So, not a direct approach.

Instead, come via a friend.

Nina Savoy.

To ingratiate itself, the Ocrassa manufactured an accidental meeting. Its first act of contact with Nina was a flurry of pheromones coupled with a casual statement of flattery. Humans couldn't resist flattery. It made them blush, even when they did not know the flatterer.

Tori Siegler was another useful entry contact into Savannah's life. The informal atmosphere at her occasional house parties was the ideal venue for a boy and girl to meet. On the evening itself, the sandwich-throat problem worked well to gain Savannah's attention and sympathy, and led naturally to the dad-with-a-knife story.

The Ocrassa talked about ticking sounds, knowing from the Horror's visits that she already made them, even if she was not aware of that yet. Talked about throats as well. About things that kept people apart. About its desire for closeness. Especially that. How difficult it was to get really close to someone, sensing Savannah never had.

No chance to increase her empathy with Reece was wasted. Little touches made it feel real: untidy bedrooms, mutual likes, shared loneliness. The throat-weapon the Ocrassa had was useless next to Savannah's, but never mind. It showed her what it had, helping to convince her that they were in this together. It worked a little more on Reece's scar as well. Made sure it didn't look recent. Made it wriggle when he talked. The Ocrassa also checked Savannah's background. Looked up her grades. Discovered how often she'd moved homes. And when it was with her it made certain it mirrored her moods precisely, reflecting her own conclusions back to her as if they were its own. Oh, weren't those monster dreams so terrifying?

And of course, whenever Savannah saw Reece with his dad, he was always affectionately tending him.

And—perhaps most important of all—to avoid any possibility of mistrust, the Ocrassa told Savannah to never, never, never allow anything near her throat.

As part of its final preparations, the Ocrassa joined Battersea running club. The track was a natural way to test Savannah's physical skills without raising her doubts.

limits of her improved eyesight.

In real darkness, she was as blind as any other human.

Useful to know.

Even so, she remained stubbornly hard to crack. The Ocrassa thought it would be easy to proceed to a lingering-enough kiss, but nature had embedded its own defense mechanisms inside Savannah Grey. She distrusted close contact with everyone, even Reece. There was no way to get near enough to her mouth. The Ocrassa created situations to do so several times, but could never get quite close enough to be sure of killing her.

Frustrated, unable to make the kiss work romantically, the Ocrassa finally changed tactics. It contrived an attack by the Horror on Reece's throat at the hospital—with the Horror doing just enough cutting. To give the episode extra authenticity, it made sure that a nurse witnessed the attack. It even underwent a real throat operation, pretending to be unconscious and sedated. It could do all these things and more without ever needing to show Savannah the extra weapons it had tucked inside Reece's body. There were many of these. Many enhancements. Things no boy could do. Waiting.

So, while it waited, it used Nina to test how close it was to success. Savannah loved Nina, so the Ocrassa ordered the Horror to take Nina to Dulwich Wood. Later, when the leaves found Savannah at the hospital, the Ocrassa accompanied her in Reece's body to Dulwich Wood. There he offered to sacrifice himself so that she could escape from the Nyktomorph and the Horror. What more heroic way to melt a human heart?

Savannah's affection for Nina ran deep, but in that tormented moment when Savannah chose Reece over Nina in Dulwich Wood, the Ocrassa knew how close it was to finally winning Savannah's heart.

Still, the Ocrassa had ordered the Horror to keep Nina. It wanted the insurance of having her in the lair. Just like the children of Mr. Gandolfo, Nina might be useful later. The Ocrassa felt it needed all such advantages against Savannah Grey. Her throat brimmed with menace. She had no idea how powerful it was.

And now the present moment. Poor Reece Gandolfo. His throat really was such a fragile thing. It might begin bleeding again at any time. The Ocrassa could easily manage a little bleeding. It could do more than that. If it wanted, it could make Reece's heart appear to stop. It could make his lungs cease to function.

All of which was needed for one reason only.

To arrive at a single point in time where Savannah, no matter what her inhibitions, could do nothing else but place her mouth over his.

To offer Reece Gandolfo her breath, a kiss of life. That point in time was now.

Savannah was above Reece.

She was still struggling to be so close to him, but she fumbled with his shirt.

Ominous noises vented from her throat, but in her passion to save him she held back the weapon. She pressed her anguished mouth to his.

And from Reece's own throat a deadly spike softly flowered and extended. The spike only drew back when Savannah hesitated. Why did she hesitate? For a moment the Ocrassa nearly opened Reece's human eyes to check. But then it sensed the shadow of Savannah's hair pass across the light, and heard her breath, and felt the ardent weight of her lips.

30

Reece's lips were soaked with blood, but I didn't care. Against every instinct, I pressed my face down, down towards his. And there followed a curiously dizzying moment, as if not only was I descending but Reece's unconscious body was heading up towards me in a rush of speed.

All I wanted to do in that moment was to breathe life back into him. But our mouths never met. My body prevented it. One of my own hands grasped the back of my head and yanked my hair with such shocking force from Reece's face that I gasped.

"Please, just this once," I begged, and during that whispered plea an object thrust in silence from Reece's lips.

It rose so swiftly that I barely had time to fling myself out of its path.

From the ground, dazed, I stared across at Reece.

He was no longer lying down. He was standing, his mouth open impossibly wide.

At first, ridiculously, I thought Reece had swallowed something. I thought an object must have become accidentally lodged in his neck, and that was why he was bleeding so badly. But then I saw a thick strand of taut flesh uncoil from inside his throat. It happened so swiftly that my old eyes would never have picked it up. The strand flicked hard, *snap*, like an elastic band, drawing the object, tool, device, whatever it was, smoothly back inside him and out of sight.

Reece did not wait for me to recover. He moved towards me—calmly, smiling as he walked—hoping that a pleasant expression coupled with my confusion might keep me there long enough to find another way to attack me.

And I was so bewildered it might have worked.

Except that my throat took charge.

There was no slow buildup of tics this time. A blistering set of drill-like noises ignited in my neck, scythed up past my teeth at an excruciatingly high pitch, and *scanned* Reece.

Reece instantly halted, suddenly looking vulnerable, human again.

I wanted so much to believe that. I wanted more than anything to believe he was human. But I knew what I'd seen, and all I could do was scream. A shriek of despair shuddered through me, mixing with the drill sounds to create a noise so loud it converted the Reece-thing's smile to fear, and made him hesitate.

It was human to hesitate.

It was human to look afraid.

I so wanted Reece to be human.

But any lingering hope I had of that vanished in the next second.

A boy would have been deafened by the noise. A boy would at least have covered his ears, raised his arms to ward me off.

Instead, glistening under the artificial night lights of the hospital corridor, new skin popped out from the Reece-thing's face. I watched in horror as the skin emerged. It jerked and stretched, first protectively covering the Reece-thing's eyes and nostrils, then anchoring itself with a crack like a staple gun to the back of the thing's head.

Terrifyingly, though, even with its eyes enclosed in all that extra skin, the Reece-thing could still see. Its face was turning, checking all the ER's entrances and exits.

Assessing the best way out.

Shaking my head, I tried to shut everything from my mind, to deny it. Reece couldn't be the monster. He couldn't be. Every fiber of my being refused to accept it. And if the Reece-thing had attacked me again in that heart-baffled moment, it might have succeeded.

But instead it set about escape.

Two wings burst through the material of Reece's denim shirt. In seconds the wings were pumped hard with blood, and the Reece-thing, fanning them, flew over the reception desk, aiming for the double-doorway exit.

I remained stunned, but my throat exploded into life. Matching the Reece-thing's movements, following it, my tongue shaped itself, targeting the fragile wings. "Please don't hurt me," the Reece-thing begged, but even if I was confused by its pleas my throat was not, and a delicate spray of noise like fine rain raked across the wing membranes.

At the same time a blunter capsule of sound discharged from my lips like a projectile. It was terrifying to feel such an unleashing of power, but I knew I needed it, required all its savagery now, and I let it go. The Reece-thing, tilting its body astonishingly fast, avoided the main blast, but the shock wave caught it just as it was flying through the ER doorway, pulverizing it against a side wall.

A boy would have been killed instantly by the blow. The Reece-thing, however, bounced off the wall and was immediately up and running. It made it out of the door, its wings shredded but still sufficiently intact to get up into the sky.

I followed it towards the exit, but my weapon was short-range and the Reece-thing had already gone beyond it. Once in open air, it squatted down on the ground, compressed its legs, and leapt—vertically—until it stood on the Golden Jubilee roof, perhaps thirty meters above.

Then it dropped out of sight on the other side of the building.

The Horror scrambled after it.

For a few seconds I just stared numbly. The rational part of me knew I should go straight after the monster, before it could retreat to its stronghold in Dulwich Wood. But at first I couldn't move. I couldn't even drag my legs forward. I could only crouch down and retch in disgust, because . . . because . . . *I'd loved him.*

The truth blasted through me.

I'd loved him. I had. A monster. I'd loved it. A monster. *A monster.*

I hunched over, my tears spilling across the pavement. *I chose you over Nina*, I thought, remembering the decision in Dulwich Wood. *I left Nina there to save you.*

I shoved my forehead into the ground, wanting to bury myself there, wanting to die. And then, as the enormity—the outrage—of what had been done to me gradually seeped into my mind, I stopped wanting to die, and instead rose to my knees.

I stood. Pushed back my hair.

Squaring my shoulders, I gazed with cold fury at the dark sky in the east.

And a new noise smoldered inside my mouth. It was like nothing that had come before. It was beauty reversed. It was purity sullied. It was every perfect bell-like chime and ravishing musical scale in this world inverted and sharpened and turned into something to break the soul.

Hearing its brutal hardness, the people closest to me backed off. Many ran. And in other circumstances I'd have closed my mouth to avoid frightening them, but that wasn't the side of me I needed to dominate now. Instead, I let it gush out, let it annihilate the brickwork of a wall in front of me. I let it flow like my own tears, let it rage. And only once I was sure I could control it and reproduce it if needed did I shut my mouth again.

I looked eastward.

I *am* alone, I thought. The Reece-thing had pretended we were in this together, but only because that wasn't true. And knowing that made it so hard to take those first steps towards Dulwich Wood. I hesitated. I couldn't help that. And then I stopped questioning my judgment, and what I should do. It wasn't my judgment that was holding me back, only fear.

What would it do if I failed? *Kill everyone in the end*, I knew instinctively. *Destroy everything.*

Stepping forward, I parted my lips, giving the noises in my throat free reign. I'd held something back until now, frightened of the consequences, but this time I did the opposite—I let all the noises loose.

And while I did so, I ran.

I traveled swiftly to the edge of Dulwich Wood. It was dark, only a half-moon tonight. Was that to my advantage or the Reece-thing's? Nothing is to my advantage here, I thought. This is its lair.

I entered the trees, and the wood again welcomed me. The birds and leaves followed me closely, like a cloak at my back, willing me on.

Shutting my mouth, I tried to prepare myself for what was to come, but that was impossible. All I could do was stay alert and try to hold my nerve. Ironically, that made me calmer. If I ever came through this, my life would be easier. My body was not my enemy. My throat, seething with energy, was under my control now, and always would be. The weapon inside was intended for a single target only.

As I stepped through the moonlit gaps among the bigger trees, I slowed down. The Reece-thing would obviously do everything in its power to trick and unnerve me. In that, though, there was also a faint ray of hope. Because surely it meant Nina wasn't dead. The Reece-thing was bound to have kept her at least half-alive for just such a moment as this—to use against me.

The near-certainty of that made my heart clench, but I contained my emotions. It wasn't emotion I needed now. How could I fight something like the Reece-thing with emotion? A startling image suddenly shot into my mind: of Nina staked out sacrificially in Dulwich Wood, with me having no better idea of how to save her than the last time I was here.

But as I entered the clearing what awaited me was the last thing I expected.

31

It was the pig-dogs. But not the alert ones from last time. They were all dead. From the state of their torn bodies, strewn across the clearing, there had obviously been a ferocious battle.

But what had killed them?

Perched in the lower branches of an oak, a solo blue eye surveyed the lifeless bodies. Had the Horror done this? No, I decided. Not enough time for it to get back from the hospital and kill so many. In any case, for all its aggressiveness, I doubted the Horror was capable of killing even a third this number on its own. Besides, it looked bewildered by the carnage. It kept glancing miserably at the pig-dogs and behind it, to a dark space between the trees.

Within that dark space, inevitably, stood the Nyktomorph.

It stood so still that the only reason I saw it at all were the gashes of blood glinting against its skin. Its whole body was besmirched with the pig-dogs' remains. Here, then, was the slayer. But why? Not for a second did I think the Nyktomorph had done this for my benefit.

"Where's Nina?" I demanded.

"The Ocrassa has taken her underground," the Nyktomorph answered impassively, shaking blood off its face.

The Ocrassa, I thought. So that's what Reece was. Not a human name. I tried to focus on that, not the boy I'd known.

"It is waiting for you," the Nyktomorph announced. "It knows you are coming. It is prepared."

Why was the Nyktomorph offering me this information? To gain my trust? To pretend it was on my side? Did it seriously expect me to believe that?

"Why did you kill the pig-dogs?" I yelled.

"I was given no specific order not to kill them," the Nyktomorph replied. "Do you understand? I was told to prepare the pig-dogs for your arrival, and show them the best attack strategy, which I did. I cannot disobey a direct command from the Ocrassa. But I have more freedom where I am not so commanded."

Studying the Nyktomorph, I had never trusted it less. One of its legs was bent, seemingly fractured, and there were gnaw-marks on its neck. What was going on here? Was the Nyktomorph pretending to be injured? Trying to lull me into believing it was weaker? That's exactly the sort of tactic the Ocrassa would use to distract me, I decided, more wary than ever.

In the end I realized that there was no way I could tell if the battle with the pig-dogs had been staged or was real. The Ocrassa could presumably set up a convincing display for me if it wanted.

"Savannah Grey," the Nyktomorph rasped, as if trying out my name for size.

"Savannah Grey," the Horror echoed meaninglessly from the tree.

I was glad to see that at least the Horror looked afraid of me, but the Nyktomorph remained unfathomable.

"I have been ordered to kill you," it said.

I shuddered. I didn't understand why it had told me this, but I nodded. Some part of me had known a battle with the Nyktomorph was unavoidable from the moment we'd met, but how was I supposed to confront a monster that revealed none of its weaknesses? I'd never even seen the Nyktomorph fight. I had no idea what it was capable of.

Glancing slowly between me and the Horror, the Nyktomorph asked quietly, "What does it mean to love?"

I refused to take the question seriously. It's delaying me, I thought. Giving the Ocrassa more opportunity to prepare.

"Where's your master?" I shouted, feeling my throat warming up.

"Nearby," the Nyktomorph replied. "And I must serve it." The Nyktomorph said this with apparent reluctance.

I trusted it even less when I saw that. "It expects your death," it told me gravely, "and I will accomplish that if I can. Do you understand what I am saying? I cannot disobey a direct command from the Ocrassa. I must genuinely try to kill you using all of my skill."

I glanced apprehensively at the Horror. It clearly wanted to attack me but was fearful. Hopping among trees, hissing softly, its arms reached alternately towards the Nyktomorph for comfort and threateningly towards me.

"*My child*," the Nyktomorph said without any prompting. "Though I did not create it, it is my responsibility."

I ignored the Nyktomorph's words. I had to get past both of them quickly.

"Has it been ordered to kill me as well?" I said, pointing at the Horror.

"Yes, but it will probably run if you attack." The Nyktomorph took a heavy step towards me. "I will fight you now," it announced. Its whole bearing was stiff with tension. "Prepare yourself, Savannah Grey."

"I don't want to fight you," I murmured, suddenly doubting myself.

The Nyktomorph almost smiled. "Do you think I will not try to kill you even so? Make no mistake, I will."

And with those words it leapt at me. A quick flick of its tail sent an S-curve rippling through its body, instantly camouflaging it. Then it lunged, its form merging against the background of grass, bushes, and starlight, a judder of speed so rapid I barely saw its outstretched teeth in time to jump aside.

The Horror, seeing an easy chance to get involved in the battle, scuttled down the tree, edging towards me.

I ignored it. I concentrated on the Nyktomorph. But even my fast-flickering eyes could barely follow as its skin merged with the darkness. It vaulted to the left, out of sight into the deep trees.

Where was it?

My eyes searched for movement, disturbances of air, an outline—anything.

I'm standing still, I realized. An easy target. Move.

Spinning on my heels, I changed position twice in as many seconds. At the same time, from my throat, came four short rising *clicks*.

Hearing them froze the Horror, but it soon sneaked forward again.

The next attack by the Nyktomorph came almost without warning. Somehow it had slipped behind my back. Only a rustle of leaves alerted me. Turning, I saw the Nyktomorph heading for me in a terrifying new way: staggered, randomly spaced leaps. The pattern was entirely unpredictable, the Nyktomorph's outline blending with tree, with sky, with whatever it passed, and as I studied what was coming, seeking a pattern in the motion *that was not there*, I knew that my eyes could not pinpoint it. My only chance was a wide blast to cover the whole area in front of me. My throat responded, building a solid wall of noise.

The Nyktomorph still nearly avoided it. Reducing its profile, pulling in its limbs to limit the target area offered, it jumped, nearly vaulting the wall before I could build it high enough. But a tangle of *clicks* exploded against its shoulder, stunning it.

The Nyktomorph pitched against a tree trunk, for a moment dazed.

And that moment was enough.

A slender, penetrating crackle flew out. Flashing like a whip from my mouth, it cut a swath through the Nyktomorph's hide.

For a few seconds the Nyktomorph remained upright, swaying, staring at itself in—what? Surprise? Disbelief? No, it was something more complex than that. Falling on its side, it tried to get back up, failed, then lay panting on the ground.

The Horror went berserk. Seeing the Nyktomorph unable to rise, it wailed and jerked twice with fright.

I ignored it. I didn't know how much damage I'd done to the Nyktomorph and, unable to take any chances, I sent another blast into its flank.

This time I tore it wide open.

The Horror screamed, its claws over its eye.

The Nyktomorph lay on the soil, still alive, but barely. It half-raised its head. It gazed at me. "You *can* kill the Ocrassa," it said, as if I was the one who needed to be persuaded of my own power.

Looking at the Nyktomorph I knew then that it was right, and I found myself falling to my knees in the mud.

"Nothing loves the Ocrassa, nor has ever done," the Nyktomorph whispered, its eyes meeting mine.

I didn't understand. The Horror bounded across the mud. Shrieking, it wiped its star-prongs across the Nyktomorph's body, trying to stuff all the lost blood back inside.

"The boy Reece is not responsible," the Nyktomorph said, from one of its last breaths. "Know that. Know he resisted as much as any human the Ocrassa has ever inhabited. But know also the Ocrassa will still use him against you if it can."

The Nyktomorph turned with difficulty to the Horror. It lifted a claw to tenderly stroke its star-prongs. The Horror blinked, then looked pleadingly at me. Any concern about its own safety was forgotten. It was suddenly only a child seeking help from wherever it could find it.

The Nyktomorph gazed up slowly. "Does it love me?" it asked, as if needing me to confirm the truth of what it was feeling.

"Yes," I said, tears streaming down my face. I didn't even know why I was crying, but nearby the Horror was also crying.

The Nyktomorph stared at me, gratitude in its eyes. It was dying, and knew it. "If you have a heart, finish this," it said. "Or I will have to get up and fight again."

"I can't," I murmured.

"You can, and it must be us both. Without me to restrain it, the Horror is only a Horror."

"I can't," I repeated, tears frozen in my eyes.

The Nyktomorph seemed startled by my compassion. And then it smiled, as if in wonderment, and with the remnants of its body scrabbled across the ground, reaching for my head.

In response, a lethal sound swooped from my throat. As it shot across the divide between us, the Horror instinctively jumped away in fright. But the Nyktomorph caught the Horror and pulled it to its chest, cradling it there.

The Horror didn't understand. It didn't know what the Nyktomorph was doing. It squealed. And then suddenly it *did* understand, and tried to break free, scraping at the Nyktomorph with its tiny arms.

But the Nyktomorph knew how to hold its own child, and gently it stroked its cheek, and at the same time the other claw of the Nyktomorph plucked the blond wig from the Horror. For a moment the Horror stared wide-eyed at the Nyktomorph—startled—its face naked and true. And then the Nyktomorph's claws closed quietly over the child's eye so it would not have to see as I carved a line of destruction through both their hearts.

32

I couldn't look at what I'd done. For a long time I could barely even raise my eyes. Then I made myself. The Nyktomorph and the Horror lay together in an embrace, piled against the leaves.

Trembling, I stared at them. I desperately needed their deaths to mean something. *Nothing loves the Ocrassa, nor has ever done.* What had the Nyktomorph meant by that? I had no idea, and rather than continue to stare at the two bodies in front of me, I wiped the blood off my jeans and headed towards the clearing.

The entrance to the lair was plainly visible. A matted set of branches loosely covered a hole in the earth. Far from avoiding me, the Ocrassa was making itself easy to find. No surprise there. No doubt it had prepared thoroughly for this moment.

The hole was wide enough for me to comfortably squeeze through—again, an invitation.

Five steep steps led to a crossing underground tunnel. It was too dark to see much beyond that. But what if the trap was here, at the entrance? Raising an arm to shield my neck, I carefully tested the crumbling earth at the brink of the hole, then jumped straight to the floor below. The smooth-walled tunnel ahead gradually descended. Beyond the first dozen meters or so, there was little light. My eyes adjusted to take in what meager chinks were available, but I was at the edge of what even my new sharper vision could handle here. Then, thinking about what lay ahead, I decided to test my throat. A series of tics simmered reassuringly, ready to explode into life when I needed them. That gave me a little more confidence, and I pressed on, thinking, *don't let me down now.*

The tunnel widened, and in a small chamber I was shocked to discover four children. Two girls and two boys, bound together with ropes. The girls were older than the boys, but they all shared similar features with each other, and with Reece. His brothers and sisters? They had to be. So those portraits I'd seen over at Reece's house had been carefully doctored to mislead me. I'd wondered why he was the same age in them all. And, looking back, hadn't the real Reece been trying to tell me something? Hadn't he shown flickers of resistance all along?

I had no idea what Reece's poor brothers and sisters were doing here, but I was wary of getting too close. There was an odd smell about them—an odor I couldn't quite identify.

All the children wore uniforms. They looked as if they'd been snatched on their way to or from school. But it must have been weeks ago because their clothes were filthy. The children were lying so still that at first I feared they were all dead. Then one of the girls stirred, crying when I shook her. *They aren't expecting me. They think I'm the Ocrassa.*

While I reassured her, the girl's sister opened her eyes, followed by the two younger boys. They were confused. They were desperately thirsty as well. They kept asking me for water, but I couldn't do anything about that. I needed to get them out as fast and as safely as possible.

Warily, I checked the ropes holding them down. The bonds were exceptionally convoluted knots that took several minutes to untie, but eventually I managed it, and the children were all able to rise and totter in front of me. One sister held the other, blinking in the darkness. The boys simply sat down again. They'd been here for so long that they couldn't grasp that this was their chance to escape.

Unprompted by me, one of them rummaged in a pocket and produced a photo. It was a snapshot of the four of them with Reece. In the photo all of them were clustered around a smiling, much younger-looking version of Mr. Gandolfo. It was harrowing gazing at the image of the healthy man he'd so recently been, but this was not the moment to tell the children what had happened to their dad.

Helping them get started, I indicated the route out and sent them gently in that direction.

Then I held my breath and prepared to go on, concentrating as I had to on the way ahead and the obvious question: why had the Ocrassa left the children here for me to find? Too busy on its way back to discover a better use for them? Possibly. But even in haste I doubted the Ocrassa made casual choices.

The tunnel descended again, the air becoming warmer, darker. My eyes compensated, but it was almost completely black now. The Ocrassa could attack me from anywhere down here, I knew. I'd barely have time to react.

So slow down. Slow down.

Edging forward, I let my mind wander back to what the Nyktomorph had told me. *The boy Reece is not responsible. Know he resisted as much as any human the Ocrassa has ever inhabited.* Remembering those words, my heart went out to Reece Gandolfo. But perhaps it was pity for myself as well, because if I killed the Ocrassa, it would be inside his body, and I couldn't separate the two, couldn't divide the boy from the monster. All sorts of emotions flared through me. Anger. Burning resentment. A deep bitterness at the loss of all the years we might have had together. How dare the Ocrassa deny me those?

Thank you for trying to help me, Reece, I thought. *I'd like to have known you. I wish I had.*

The only change in the next few minutes was that the tunnel narrowed and my mouth started to feel dry. The air down here lacked moisture, but I didn't think that could account for it. I licked my lips and swallowed, but it made no difference.

Unable to understand the reason, but feeling no pain, I walked tentatively on.

Ahead of me, the tunnel broadened again, and I found myself in another wide chamber. I slowed. The Ocrassa was close. I knew that not because I could hear it, but because a trace of maleness—Reece's scent—tainted the air.

I shuddered, ignoring it. Peering ahead, I carefully checked the ceiling. Barely a mote of light penetrated these depths. Wasn't this dangerous for the Ocrassa, too? How could it see me? Then I remembered its eye-shields.

Of course. It didn't need light. It could hunt me blind.

As I crouched down in the chamber, letting that terrible realization sink in, I was suddenly overcome with fear. There was almost no chance of leaving these tunnels alive. Even so, I had to go on. This was doubtless my only chance to kill the Ocrassa. It knew me too well now to ever let me get this close again. And if I failed, I knew there was no one to take my place.

But even knowing that for a moment, I was overwhelmed, paralyzed by uncertainty, trembling at the edge of the light. Because of course there was another direction I could go, wasn't there? Back. I could retreat. Leave the way I'd come. I knew a great deal about the Ocrassa now. Perhaps enough to stay ahead of it. If I left this part of the country altogether, changed my identity, altered my appearance, maybe I could evade it for months, years even.

Perhaps a lifetime.

I stood still, rigid with fear, the choice to go on so appalling that for a moment I couldn't do so.

Then I made myself lean ever so slightly into the darkness ahead. Lifted my right foot. Just that. Pressed it forward. *Come on.* Took the tiniest step. *Come on.* Another.

The third footstep led towards a freshening of air, a new chamber—and something that made me gasp.

It was Nina. Her ghostlike body was suspended from ropes attached to the ceiling at the back of the chamber.

I stifled a cry. She didn't know I was there. I'd been treading so cautiously that she hadn't heard me. Good. I needed time to calm myself before I approached. If there were any booby traps, what better place than here, triggered as I attempted to free her?

The knots binding Nina were more of the same complex variety used on the children. This time, though, Nina's mouth was gagged with cloth as well—as if the Ocrassa wanted to make sure she stayed silent. Why? The same indistinct but cloying odor I'd smelled on the children surrounded her. But it was much more pungent here. I sniffed it nervously.

Never taking my eyes off the chamber walls, I painstakingly loosened the knots. "Shush, it's OK," I whispered as Nina, feeling me there, twisted and turned.

Flexing her arms, mouthing hysterically through the gag, she kept urgently trying to say something. I moved on to the gag as fast as I could, but it was even harder to undo, the knots were so intricate.

As soon as the last knot was undone Nina spat the cloth from her mouth. "It put something on the ropes!" she croaked. "It was here a while ago, rubbing in a chemical."

"What?"

"Test your throat," Nina wheezed. "Test it!"

I coughed. No reaction. The tics fell dead on my tongue.

My throat was numb. Frozen.

Anesthetized.

No! My heart instantly slammed into overdrive, hammering in my chest.

"Hold on to me," I rasped. I was barely able to get even those words out, my neck muscles were so crippled. Knowing my only chance of getting us out alive now was to run, I flung Nina across my shoulder and headed as fast as I could back up the tunnel.

Could I make it? My body was already starting to purge the chemicals from my throat, but the Ocrassa, of course, did not wait for that. It must have long ago chosen this as the optimal moment to attack.

From the tunnel below there came the heavy sound of something uncoiling. My mind spasmed in fear as I heard the Ocrassa smash through a connecting wall. I adjusted Nina on my shoulder, but she was an awkward size for the tunnel. Carrying her in the confined space was holding me up—as no doubt the Ocrassa knew it would.

"Pull your arms in! Away from the walls!" I shouted.

The earth shifted as the Ocrassa erupted from a side tunnel to my left. I tried to estimate how far away it was. If I could make it outside, get to the surface, I might have a chance. The tunnel narrowed again, and I felt hot breath on the hairs of my arms. A wave of panic cut through me, but I didn't look back. I knew that's exactly what the Ocrassa wanted me to do.

Clinging to Nina, I reached the point where I'd come across the four children. The entrance was directly ahead, a patch of moonlit earth, achingly close. I scrambled over loose, trampled soil, for a mind-numbing second losing my footing. Then I found the steps.

A leap into the night air.

Coughing out stale tunnel dust, I burst onto the surface, into the clearing.

Leaves immediately surrounded me and Nina like a shroud, blurring the edges of our forms. Other leaves stuffed the entrance, forcing the Ocrassa to fight its way out. I hurriedly placed Nina on the grass behind me, but even before I turned back to the tunnel entrance something was springing through the matted branches.

Howling winds blasted it, but they barely held the Ocrassa back.

Its head emerged first, then its neck. As I made myself turn to face it, I somehow expected to see an object of many terrors—something vast and confident and utterly alien—but of course the Ocrassa was still in the Reece-persona. What I saw was not a monster, but a face I'd loved. *And it wants that. It wants me to see the boy, to make me hesitate.*

The Ocrassa hauled itself out of the tunnel, and every step of the way the wind and leaves furiously attacked it.

To combat them the Ocrassa sealed its mouth and nostrils.

How long before my throat recovered? Several more minutes, I realized. Could the leaves obscure me from the Ocrassa for that long? No. It was heading inexorably towards me, only the thrashing winds delaying it.

"Hi, Savannah," it said, the words cutting through a slash in its mouth. "How're you feeling?"

I didn't answer. I knew it was only trying to get me to talk so it could estimate the damage to my throat and pinpoint precisely where I was amid the leaves.

"That bad?" it said, halving the distance between us. "Then you won't be able to fight, will you? What about Nina? You think she's still alive? You think you saved her? I killed her while you were running through the tunnel. You didn't even notice, did you? Take a look."

It required all of my strength not to glance behind me. Whether or not the Ocrassa was telling the truth, I knew its purpose was to throw me into turmoil.

And then something unexpected happened. The Ocrassa faltered. It stood still. Took a step back. And for one heart-wrenching moment I knew, because there could be no other explanation, that something—someone—was resisting it, trying to help me.

Reece.

The Ocrassa immediately beckoned to a shadow in the trees above. A huge apelike creature dropped down, placing its lips against Reece's. The essence of the Ocrassa was being transferred to a more reliable vessel, and if I'd understood that truth a fraction of a second earlier I might have been able to catch the Ocrassa between bodies.

My blow came just too late. I launched myself from the leaves, and with all of my strength struck the ape-thing's head. The Ocrassa was almost instantly in control of its new ape-body, but my blow was so immense that I knocked it back. And the damage was appalling. Its ape-nose was completely wiped out, plus its left cheek and its eye on that side.

But it rose again. This was no ordinary ape. It was clearly a creation of the Ocrassa's intended for just this moment. It stood, lifted its grizzled chin—and headed forward.

Winds pummeled it from all directions, but it drove through the blasts.

I shivered as another eye slid into the gap of the Ocrassa's new face, replacing it. Around us the leaves crackled, and the moon suddenly shone down.

What now? I had just hit the Ocrassa with as much force as I could deliver, but it was largely unaffected.

Realizing that it had survived my best blow, it looked more confident as well. And, of course, it had discovered exactly where I was.

Reece lay on the ground, barely moving.

I looked away from him, at the muscular ape. An unsteady *tic-tic* flared in my neck, but it was still pathetically weak. Could I outrun the Ocrassa? No.

It was no more than two body lengths from me now. Despite that, it was taking no chances, and another membrane, like a shaped shield, flicked from its mouth, instantly hardening over its entire ape-head.

At the same time it dove for my throat.

I couldn't avoid it any longer. All I could do was snatch the Ocrassa's wrists together in mid-flight—and abruptly we were slammed together, strength on strength, our bodies shuddering at the impact.

Less than a second later a slim probe emerged from the pupil of the Ocrassa's left eye. Only my extraordinary reaction speed enabled me to avoid it as it stabbed at my face. The probe retracted, then lunged again. I evaded it a second time, but it kept shifting extraordinarily fast, trying to predict my head movements. I was conscious that we were in a dance of death, but one so fast that anything else on this world would have seen us as nothing but a blur of joined heads.

As if to prove this, Nina stood up in what appeared to be slow motion. She lifted one ponderous foot, running towards me as fast as she could, but it was still an impossibly sluggish action. To the left of her, the freed Reece was also beginning to rise to his knees.

The Ocrassa ignored them, adjusting to my head movements. It was better at adapting than I was. It was in every way stronger, more prepared, more poised, more perfect a weapon. I continued to shift my head rapidly, but I couldn't move fast enough to avoid the probe indefinitely. And in the end it . . . touched my neck. Just a smear of the skin, but that was enough. The probe didn't need to go deep.

Puncturing a surface vein, it injected something into my bloodstream.

I knew the moment it flooded inside me that it was the *Ocrassa itself* that was entering my body. As it poured down my veins I knew also that I couldn't stop it. It was too quick, too flexible, too experienced. My own blood responded, but not fast enough to destroy what was being forced inside.

Both our bodies gradually slowed down: mine because I had no choice, the Ocrassa because the larger part of it that was still inside the ape-thing was now content simply to hold me securely and wait. Our faces were locked together in what to Nina, still running towards me incredibly slowly, must have looked like a lover's clinch. She screamed, and at the speed I was still reacting, the sound lengthened into a howl that went on and on.

The Ocrassa gradually started to take control of my neck. Nerve centers were shattered, and seconds later I knew my throat would never be a serious weapon again—in other words, that I had lost, that it was over.

But the Ocrassa wanted to make sure, and its probe reached for control of my brain.

For some reason, although I knew the Ocrassa was about to possess me, in that moment, I took the time to look around. Birds were screeching, attacking the Ocrassa, without effect. To my left, the Horror and the Nyktomorph lay in their own beautiful embrace. The four sisters and brothers were huddled against a tree, too tired and bewildered to do anything except hold each other up against the wind. Nina was still traveling forward as well, one incredibly slow step at a time. And behind her came Reece. Running, crying as he ran, he roared my name, tears slipping with almost magical slowness down his face.

And above me, and around me, were the leaves and the birds of Dulwich Wood. I was surrounded by them. Surrounded by nature. I knew I only had moments to live as a girl, and yet in those last snatched few seconds, I felt a vast, quiet, stirring love for life in all its gladdening variety around me. All this time I'd felt so alone, but gazing up I knew that I wasn't alone at all, and never had been. Nature was everywhere. It flowed and swept and wept inside me. The leaves were subtle raptures. I felt a connectedness with every mysterious thing, perfect and imperfect. I was the slow upraising of mountains. I was jubilant seas. I was every soft mouth, and every lost child knocking at a door, waiting for someone to hear.

And then, with the Ocrassa gathering inside me, spreading a black bulge and canvas across my mind, I turned back to look at the ape-thing.

Its face was close, but of course the Ocrassa was no longer seeking a kiss. It was no longer seeking anything. It needed only to wait until it had control of my brain. Then it could transfer itself from the ape to me.

The Ocrassa's consciousness reached the center of my mind, and the first thing I saw . . . was Reece.

The true Reece, the beautiful boy. I saw him utterly, I saw him exposed. I saw his soul, saw everything he had tried to do to stop the Ocrassa. I even saw the lost kisses. So many kisses we'd missed, so many I might have offered back to him. But it was OK. There were more kisses in Reece's eyes, there were always more kisses, his eyes said, and suddenly I knew that if I made it through this we would always be together. And wanting that more than anything, I turned to look at him, so that if I was about to die at least my last moments would be spent gazing into his lovely face.

The Ocrassa reached the final part of my mind. The part containing my deep emotions.

And this time I was ready. I was waiting for it there. I did not resist it. I let it in.

Nothing loves the Ocrassa, nor has ever done.

I flooded my mind with love. But not love of nature. Nor of life in general, nor even Nina. I filled it with love of a boy, of Reece. I saturated my mind with that wondrous moment at the hospital just before I'd tried so hard to kiss him, when all I'd wanted to do was take away his suffering and give him everything.

And the Ocrassa—hesitated.

It paused. Dallied in my mind, astonished. It did not know what turbulence had suddenly robbed it of equilibrium in this tender, love-disturbed place. It only knew that it wanted to linger there.

And while it did so, its ape-mouth gaping in wonder, my throat quietly stirred. A secret splinter of sound stole out. Shush, I said lovingly, holding the Ocrassa inside the ape with the love in my breath. And while it waited, patiently, curiously, the splinter sank inside the Ocrassa's trusting lips, and smoothly eased open its throat.

The Ocrassa had one long moment to look into the full depth of my eyes for the love it expected to see there before it realized what had been done to it. And then the splinter found its ribs, nudged them deftly aside, and ripped out its heart.